The Road to Discovery

MICHAEL CHUKWUDI

PHOENIX VOICES PUBLISHING

Foreword

The Road to Discovery is a creative work of arts designed and produced by Michael Chukwudi to unfold the mysteries borne on human debility. One is exposed to a lifestyle which may not be conventionally acceptable because of pride, ego, envy, humiliation, foolishness and their likes.

A critical summary of the book proves the underlying effect of barrenness in an African setting of the story. Anulika represents the suffering masses who are plunged into a societal demeanor of culture, associations, tradition and ethos in the communities. Such beliefs and norms call for reformation.

It takes people like Anulika to bridge the gap between the old and the modern system of life endeavour. A girl so determined to make her future being fruitful in spite of odds that enveloped her at tender age when she lost her parents to death. In the old system there was no difference between barrenness and female-child bearing. They are tied with the same knot; but in the presence: modernism, there are tremendous changes that a female is as good as the male child, except on one (The one is for you to brainstorm).

Modernism is a way of reformation through education and its facts. It is a pathway to enlightenment. It builds up understanding to create love, happiness, peace and unity. The development in any society cannot be void of these abstracts.

Ejikeme and his beloved wife, Nwanyimma had no formal education. Illiteracy was their thorn in flesh even as best farmers in the whole community of Amagwu. They were humiliated for lack of a male child who would become the hire of the family. Anulika was their only child who depicts degraded quality because she was a girl. Nwanyimma's barrenness before she finally had a female child was bitterly expressed. She commented, *"How long? Ages? Eternity? Or in the graveyard? {'m beginning to lose my patience. I want to carry my own child that I'll enjoy the beauty of marriage. Perhaps, the joy of parenting. Everybody will know at least I'm not a witch as they refer to me"*. She was banished for some years because she fought a woman who insulted her. It was a taboo in the land for a barren woman to fight a woman who has a child.

Barrenness could lead to disassociation and banishment, and cold wars among brothers. It leads to polygamy to avoid childlessness in a family, particularly for a male child. Thanksgiving to their gods was necessary after a bountiful harvest that pleased them. Custom permits ladies and girls to dress in attractive and modest apparels to be admired by suitors who would marry them. Oh! Multiple funny things to lure a brother on a lady he never proposed to marry. What an interesting paradise of proverbs and idioms to fancy this work.

It is good to learn from those who knew better. Illiteracy may be eradicated only when the educated are encouraged to deliver their talents to those who need them. An illiterate leader would always arrogate himself undue privileges over the

v

educated who is well informed on the matter. Igwe of Amagwu, King Ogueji, is a good example of them who ignorantly could lead their subjects to the ditch. Take a habit of transforming your darkness to light.

Leadership that cannot positively influence your society must be dropped and replaced. Leadership is a privilege not a right. Anulika was dropped as poor and wretched orphan yet her stride to education exposed her to the world. She refused to compromise her background. Her prospect and vision for life were not ruined. She was known to the world as a medical practitioner who invented drugs to cure Lassa Fever.

The story focuses on culture, tradition, and norms in Amagwu. They believed on spells as apportioned by their gods on the people as nemesis. The leaders' blood streams are full with bribery and corruption as they avert the truth but promote injustice. The book is good and I recommend it for your reading and studies.

Ikhechi G., Owabie University of Ibadan, Ibadan

Reviews

Blurbs from different literary critics in support of the work

    1. *The Road to Discovery* is an innovative pathway for the youths of this 21st century.

Prof. C.V. Nnamani. Former, HOD Department of Applied Biology,

Ebonyi State University, Nigeria.

    1. ...enthralling, yet the inner core sometimes leaves you sad as it also draws your attention to the very realities of a society...

Ofonime Inyang, PhD, Former General Secretary, Association of Nigerian Authors (ANA)

    1. Michael C. Ikegwu's "*The Road to Discovery,*" is a story of courage and dreams that flows through panoramas of pain and hardship in which human condition is constructed, dissected, and depicted. It is a journey inside the infinite shades of emotions that move and change the world - a journey worth sharing and diving into. Michael's capturing words

mesmerize, shout, whisper, and transport with rhythm and emotion into an intricate universe, our own.

Michal Musialowski, Scholar of Nigerian poetry and a poet, English Department Leibniz University Hannover, Germany.

1. This book is recommended especially for youths and parents.It reveals a typical life situation where poverty and ignorance have hindered the development of the society. It is therefore an eye-opener to our contemporary society. Nothing good comes easy but 'He who opens a school door closes a prison'.

Sr. Nora Obianuju Ubadiniru Principal, Divine Love
Secondary School, Trans-Ekulu

1. Michael Chukwudi takes a bold step into questioning the societal norm hinged on male dominance.

Opia-Enwemuche Maxwell O. Author of 'The Oracle of Isieke and Diary of a Keke Driver.

Chapter One

It was a bright cold evening in May in the nineties. Nwanyimma sat in front of a musky, damp, mud house with a thatched roof. The wind would rush through the holes in the window, leaving the door to hang on its hinges at a jaunty angle. Mazi Udemba's house outlasted every home in the Amagwu-nze village. Mazi Udemba's house was built with original materials.

She was in her early forties and tall. Her chocolate skin began to turn darker due to a lack of proper maintenance and as usual, Africa's harsh weather. She sat on a brown old wooden chair on the front porch of the hut; wearing a yellow sleeveless blouse tied wrapper that extended to her knees. She carried an old calabash on her lap. The calabash contained melon seeds. As she peeled off the seed coatings, she couldn't help but stare at the birds chirping and flying to and fro; as if they were looking for prey to devour. She held her face forward in a steady, palpable, authoritative gaze.

Nwanyimma sat beating her legs in intervals to scare away and kill off the mosquitoes. These mosquitoes have grown to be the size of houseflies, buzzing around looking to land on and bite her ears. Nwanyimma would clap *kpam, kpam* to kill the mosquitoes. A mosquito landed on Nwanyimma's leg, sucking her blood. She swatted it dead then cleaned the blood on her legs. Nwanyimma then continued to peel the melon seed coatings.

Soon enough, a rat passed by her hut side. "Bingo," she called. Bingo, her dog lay close to the old kitchen site which is a stone's throw from the hut. She signaled to Bingo "*shi, shi,*" pointing toward the direction of the rat. Bingo's predatory instincts kicked in. She went for the kill, diving toward the rat. The rat skirted into the bushes near the hut, while Bingo watched. She then returned to her previous location to lie. Check.

Not long enough, Ejikeme, Nwanyimma's husband came through the narrowing path that led to his medieval hut. Ejikeme is a tall, middle-aged man with an average-built body. He has a large mustache and in his chieftaincy wear made from the skin of a lion, or isiagu as it was colloquially called. Ejikeme has an oblong face with angular cheekbones and a pointed chin. His dark eyes were small and spaced evenly apart; sitting below his bushy eyebrows. Ejikeme held his gnarled wooden staff in his right hand. As he walked, the staff made a knocking sound in intervals; *kpom, kpom*. Bingo saw Ejikeme and rose; running towards him with her tail wagging. Ejikeme ignored Bingo's greetings. The expression on his face explained his mood. Bingo went back and laid down.

She dropped the calabash on the floor, poured back the melon seeds on her hand, and sighed "ewo!" she re-tied her wrapper as she stood to welcome her husband. With her cosmic smile, she moved to greet him, but he was mute. He walked past her. Nwanyimma felt uneasy as this is the first time her lovely husband ignored her. This did not faze her though because she believed that no matter how unpleasant things are, she will find a way to put things back in order. Nwanyimma stood with her mouth open, gazing at nothing as all kinds of thoughts ran through her mind. She watched him walk away, head low, shoulders slumped.

Ejikeme slammed the door angrily and directly sat on the reclining chair, leaning backward. Nwanyimma stood outside for a moment, and carried by her deep concern for her husband's unconventional attitude, she stepped into the house.

She went to a small room in the hut and got water from the earthen pot. The water was cold from the weather. She squatted and gave her husband the cup with a warm welcome. Ejikeme stretched out his dark-skinned hand and drank the water, thanking his wife. Nwanyimma squatted by Ejikeme, yearning to hear the mystical news that changed his demeanor. She collected the cup and kept it inside a basket near her. Ejikeme took his wife into his arms as if to reassure her that all is well. He learned a long time ago to love his wife even in the thickest of fog. Those thin arms of his weren't enough to calm her anxiousness. Tears already formed in her eyes and began to drip down.

Nwanyimma desperately kept asking herself "What could've gone wrong?" Every second of her husband's muteness removed a bit from her brain.

Ejikeme cleaned the tears with his right thumb and took a brief breath. *Hum*, he looked up the old thatched roof and down the mud floor, and then he turned to his wife. He was yet to tell her what the ordeal was. Nwanyimma waited for some minutes to hear from him. She then became impatient, she stood up, retied her wrapper, strode to the window, and stood mute with her hands crossed as she looked at the bushy back of the hut; waiting for her husband to talk.

He watched her stand then got up and held her hand, "*Nkem*, I'm so sorry for having acted the way I did earlier."

She hopefully thought that her husband would tell her what the problem is. Nwanyimma demanded to know what brought about that bitter attitude of her husband.

She looked at him, used a low tone, and said.

"*Nkem*, I think it's better to tell me what made you so infuriated." she added, "Perhaps, the problem shared is half solved. Remember, I'm your wife and I ought to know what's eating you up".

Ejikeme touched by his wife's words like a child forced a word from his mouth, he told her that his older brother and the elders had been the bone in his throat.

Still confused, she said to him, "*Nkem*, make me understand. What has your older brother done this evening?"

Ejikeme took a brief breath again, looked at his wife, and reminded her of the promise they made before they married, he could only state that; "Even in the dreaded moments, in hardship, and in good times, we should not relent nor let what they say affect the way we see ourselves." This time, he drew her closer, and they embraced.

She still had no notion of what message her husband wanted her to hear, but without a doubt, his words were meant to prepare her for the news she wouldn't embrace.

With a low-pitched voice, he told her "The elders, including my only brother, told me that you are barren. They gave me the ultimatum that I should remarry, or else they will ban me from associating with them. Nevertheless, what exasperated me the most was when my older brother Ikeobi told me that 'I've no one who'll answer my father's name, someone who'll inherit my property, not even a mere female child that'll take care of us at an old age'."

With a furious voice that took the high notes of a prolonged, painful squeal, she called the gods to know why they abandoned her. She talked to the gods as if they were there with her.

"Gods of my forefather, what did I do wrong to deserve all this? At least, I lived my life trying to please you by preserving my virginity until marriage." she sobbed as she spoke in anger.

Ejikeme tried to put her together and told her the gods will one day remember them.

Out of pain, she shouted "How long? Ages, eternity, or in the graveyard? I'm beginning to lose my patience. I want to carry my child and enjoy the beauty of marriage and perhaps the joy of parenting; so that everybody will know at least I'm not a witch as they refer to me."

Ejikeme tried to calm her down and raised his voice, "Enough *nkem*, at least I'm not complaining and will never do, let us just hope. One day, the gods will bless us with a child. Nevertheless, who are we to question the gods in their makings? Mortals like us?" he hugged her tightly, her head tie brushed against his chin.

It was already six-thirty in the evening, and she left to prepare food for her husband, believing that one day the gods will indeed remember them as her husband assured. She prayed it happens soon to surprise and dumbfound her foes.

* * *

Two days later, it was about six 0'clock in the morning and the birds were awake speaking in a high-pitched staccato. It was a cold odd morning. The darkness still covered the sky in the Amagwu-Nze village. It was the time of the year when the nights were longer and days shorter. Nwanyimma hurriedly woke up from her old bed made of bamboo trees, a mat, and a wrapper spread on the top; softening the surface for a relaxed sleep. Ejikeme was still sound asleep snoring *hu, hu, hu*. He wore an old shirt and black trousers. He covered himself with a wrapper because of the cold weather. Nwanyimma sat at the edge of the bed with her legs on the floor. She tied a wrapper that extends from her chest to her knees and put on a sweater. She tapped

Ejikeme to stop him from snoring. He turned but still feeling sleepy, answered each time she tapped him with an *ee, ee, ee*. Ejikeme went back to his early morning sleep. Nwanyimma stood up, and strode to the window, arms crossed across her chest, she was cold. She stood beside the old window covered with a wrapper to prevent the cold air from rushing in as usual. She pulled down the wrapper a little to allow enough light so that she can prepare the morning meal. There was much work to do at the farm.

The atmosphere was dark causing her to soliloquize, "Why is the atmosphere so dark, but the cock is already telling us that it's early morning and to begin the day's work? *Hum*!" she exclaimed, "It's the gods that have an explanation for my questions." she added.

Ejikeme was wriggling on his bamboo bed as he snored.

Nwanyimma stood agape gazing at nothing; listening to the cheerful songs of the birds. He rolled over on his bed and stretched his arms high above his head onto the cold mud floor, brushing his hand against the old lantern. Ejikeme reached for his wife but she wasn't on the bed.

He got up and exclaimed, "*Ewo*!" thank the gods it's yet another day."

Hearing his voice, she turned and greeted her husband, "*Nkem ututu oma* (good morning Nkem)." they exchanged pleasantries while Ejikeme was still on the edge of the bed with his hands placed on the bed.

He demanded to know why his wife woke up that early.

Asking in a lovely low tone he said, "*Nkem*, why are you denying yourself sleep on this cold, lovely morning? Come back to bed." he stretched his hands and gestured for her to come back.

She smiled and told him "It's already the morning, the birds are chirping to the gods. The cock has already crowed for the fifth time, I need to get the food ready and get going. At least, it's our first time going to the farm after the first rain from the gods." she waited, motioned, and continued; "Maybe you forgot that the earlier you work, the earlier you finish." She added.

Ejikeme smiled at his wife's gestures and insisted that she still needs some rest to be able to work at the farm. She went back reluctantly to bed. Ejikeme laid back while she sat gazing at the old thatched roof of the hut.

At about seven O'clock in the morning, she set to go to the farm with Ejikeme. She tied a wrapper that extends to her knees, wore a long sleeve, tied a scarf around her waist, and carried a basket. Inside the basket were a machete, a small hoe, food in a calabash, and a jar of water. She stood with certitude waiting for Ejikeme who was still inside the hut. After waiting a few minutes, she became impatient. The only thing she could think to do was the farm work. She was a hardworking woman who was never tired until she finished her chores.

She raised her voice calling her husband, "*Nkem*, please be fast we need to get going so that we'll finish the work at the farm before the rain starts falling, you know too well that we are in the rainy season."

Ejikeme who was still inside the hut came out with a hoe placed on his shoulder. He wore an old singlet, shorts, and a hat on his head that covered his forehead. Ejikeme bent his head as he walked through the door to avoid hitting his head on the edge.

"*Nkem*, please don't be mad at me I was trying to get ready," he said softheartedly as he gave his wife a suiting smile.

"Let's get going since you're already done," she said smiling back at him.

Ejikeme reminded her that he'll be stopping by to see Mazi Udoka to negotiate when he'll come to help them with the farm work. Mazi Udoka's hut was just a few meters walk from Ejikeme's compound. They both set to the farm. Bingo got up, wagged her tail, and followed them. Nwanyimma motioned to Bingo to go back but she was eager to head to the farm that day.

After several attempts to make Bingo go back home, Ejikeme told his wife she can come.

"Who knows, the dog will catch a squirrel for us today," he said smiling.

With a low tone, she replied, "*Nkem*, who'll look after the house? You and I know that she had been a good watchdog!"

"Gods of our fathers will watch in our absence," Ejikeme snapped.

They both smiled and continued walking to the farm as they talked.

She exclaimed as though something came to her mind, "*Chei*! *Nkem*, do you still remember that this year is the harvest of the gods?"

"Oh!" Ejikeme shouted, "I almost forgot, that reminds me, our crops will do well this season," he added.

"Well, well," she said with enthusiasm, "when we harvest, we'll take a bountiful quantity to the gods to give thanks. Importantly, we'll ask them to bless us with our children," she said worriedly.

"*Nkem*, you worry a lot, they'll surely bless us when it's time, and soon enough, they'll surely answer our prayers," Ejikeme reassured.

"I see!" she replied worriedly.

They walked for about ten poles and got to Udoka's hut. The hut's entrance was too narrow, and it has farms to the right and left. The farm belonged to Udoka's wife Adaego.

"*Nkem*, you will be going with Bingo while I see Udoka so that I can talk about the work with him," Ejikeme said.

"Do not waste time so we'll finish the work early," she said softly.

"Yes, *nkem*", he replied.

"*Ngwa* Bingo, *uje*," she said to Bingo.

She left with Bingo while the husband took the entrance to Udoka's hut. Bingo was running at the front while she followed her at the back.

Adaego sat on the verandah of the old hut. Adaego is a short, overweight, woman in her fifties. Her hair was neatly plaited with local thread. She sat on an old wooden chair with a tray of local rice, separating the chaffs from the rice by blowing air continuously on the tray when suddenly Ejikeme came in.

Seeing him, she greeted,

"*Ututu oma nwoke mara mma.*" he is fondly called this by the villagers. Although Ejikeme is a handsome man in his late forties, she wondered how handsome he was in his youth.

"*Nneoma, ututuoma,*" he replied.

Adaego raised her voice to call her son Jidenna to get a seat for their visitor. Ten-year-old Jidenna ran out from the hut wearing shorts with many patches. The patched holes still exposed parts of his buttocks, and allowed for gas to pass freely whenever he farts because of this, his friends keep ridiculing him.

"*Nne*, you called me?" he asked.

"Yes! Get a seat for our visitor," she replied.

He was about to go when Adaego called him back,

"*Bia*!" she shouted, "You don't know how to greet again or is it part of what you've been learning from those stupid friends of yours?"

Feeling shy this time, he turned, covered his face with one of his hands, and greeted

"*Ututuoma Nna anyi,*"

"*Ututuoma nwam, kedu*?" Ejikeme replied.

"*Odimma,*" Jidenna replied.

"He's only a small boy, with time he'll change, please do not scold him this way again," Ejikeme said warmly.

"Oh!" she shouted, small boy? His mates have given birth to two children," she said shouting at Jidenna to go inside and get a chair. Jidenna went in lackadaisically to get the chair.

"Married?" Ejikeme probed. "What does this age know about marriage? It's child abuse," he added.

Jidenna brought the chair, kept it on the floor, and dusted it with his right hand "*kpam, kpam.*"

"Nnam you can now sit," he said.

"Thank you so much, my son," Ejikeme said as he threw a friendly slap across his shoulder, and sighed as he bent to sit.

"*Ewo*! The gods of our fathers,"

Adaego with her mouth opened to her jaw gazed at Ejikeme while he tried to sit on the wooden chair.

Ejike's wife walked for about ten poles and came across mama Ifenyinwa, the wife of Mazi Ikeobi, and the only older brother of Ejikeme. She's tall, dark, and has an average body build. She wore a short sleeve blouse, with a tied wrapper that extended to her elbows. She heads to the farm with a basket relaxed on her head and her hands on her sides without supporting the basket.

On seeing her, Ejike's wife greeted her, "*Ututuoma nwunyedi m,*"

With her devil-may-care outlook and stellar smile, she passed without responding to the greeting. Ejike's wife was so curious to know what brought about the rough but bitter manner of mama Ifenyinwa.

"*Nwunyedi m*, I'm greeting *o*!" she said the second time.

Like a lion making an uproar, mama Ifenyinwa shouted, "*O gini*! *Amosu nwanyi*, what's so good about this morning *eeh*?" she said as though they've been quarreling for ages.

"*Nwunyedi m* what have I done to you to deserve this barbarous attitude of yours early this morning? Nevertheless, I greeted you when I saw you," she asked surprisingly with her mouth opened to her jaw.

Mama Ifenyinwa in her aggressive manner, and with the basket still relaxed on her head, clapped her hands, displaying what she said.

"Stop it, you sycophant," mama Ifenyinwa said angrily. "You pretend to be who you're not," she added. "Why don't you let us live the way we've been before the witch breeze blew you to our family?"

Still surprised, she demanded to know what'd have brought about the aggressiveness and nonchalant attitude of mama Ifenyinwa. She paused, shook her head in surprise, and continued;

"But mama Ifenyinwa if I may ask, what exactly is the problem? Tell me. Let us settle them amicably."

"Mama amicable, you think you know how to blow big grammar *eeh*?" she shouted, "You should use that big grammar to get pregnant instead of bewitching all in this family. Nevertheless, you and I know we're both illiterates, it baffles me to see that you're now blowing big grammar."

"Mama Ifi, why not tell me what I've done? Let me correct myself than insulting me this early morning," she replied furiously.

"No! No! Stop it, why do you always pretend as if you don't know what you've done?" Mama Ifenyinwa shouted. "You bewitched your husband to talk to my own good-looking and charming husband any way he decides?"

She was intensely violet as wind or storm; she drew closer to her, "it's high time you left to your family because your presence in this family is no longer recognized." She Points at Bingo that sat on the narrowing path waiting for Ejike's wife. She said, "That's where you belong. She's just barren just like you. One day, the air will blow, and the buttocks of the hen will expose."

Ejike's wife was goaded by anger said, "Mama Ifenyinwa, I'll not have you insult me." Before she could finish talking, mama Ifi as she was colloquially called cut in.

"What will happen? Tell me, will you fight me? I won't need the gods' help with the person I'll defeat," she said boastfully.

"Mama Ifenyinwa, I'm only respecting you, but it seemed you never deserved my respect."

Stormed by anger, mama Ifi raised her hands and struck her with a sound like the cracking of a bullwhip.

"Who do you think you are to talk to me any way you like? I married into this family before you," she added.

Ejike's wife paused her lips, raised her hands back, and threw her hand forward as strongly as she could, slapping her in the face. The crack of her hand contacting her skin echoed off in the air. Without a moment of hesitation, mama Ifi retied her wrapper more firmly, removed her foot wears and jumped Ejike's wife. Unfortunately, Ejike's wife overpowered her. Soon enough, she was already on the ground. Ejike's wife was on top of her teaching her a lesson she'll never dare to forget. Bingo was running in every nook and cranny of the road looking for help. Mama Ifi was on the floor shouting profusely and swearing from the ordeal with Ejike's wife. She managed to get up and thank the gods for the two maidens Ekemma and Adaobi for coming back to the stream. Ekemma balanced a bucket of water on her head while Adaobi had a brimming water pail balanced on her head supported by her left hand and talked with her right.

On seeing the two women, they suddenly dropped the water and ran on their heels to separate them. They scramble to help the two women end their fight and succeeded in doing so. When mama Ifi got up, she was badly bruised and injured.

She picked up her basket and helped her put it on her head as she walked away promising Ejike's wife that she'll answer the elders for fighting her. It was never new in the history of Amagwu-Nze village that barren women were not to fight mothers with children. Barren women in Amagwu-Nze were *osu, or* outcasts as they believed. They all believed that either the women or their mothers wronged the gods and in turn, they decided to block their wombs. Ejike's wife, Ekemma, Adaobi, and Bingo left their different ways.

The family hut had only one entrance that was about one meter wide. She got to the hut, and her husband; Mazi Ikeobi sat on a reclining chair eating his food. Mazi Ikeobi is a lightskinned man in his late fifties. His square and heavy-set jaw was eternally set in a smirk; confining the lines of his mischievous eyes, which glittered with a self-pride of a man who thinks himself to be the best in Amagwu-Nze. He had a big *akpu bolus* he was about to swallow when he saw his wife crying as she marched towards the hut. He managed to swallow the *akpu bolus*, struggling with it to pass through his tiny but big throat that had expanded because of the constant swallows that are big enough to feed five children.

"What?" he shouted as he rose from the chair with unwashed hands.

When his wife got to the verandah of the hut, she dropped the basket balanced on her head, stood as she slouched, and cried bitterly with indiscipline as though she lost a son. Her husband tried to get a better grasp of her, but she shouted a cry like a child.

"It is that barren witch that your brother married from Akpuato,"

"*Ewo!*" shouted Ikeobi with his mouth wide agape, that witch of a barren woman?

"Yes *o, Nna anyi!*" she replied.

"*Aru!*" shouted Ikeobi, "She forgot the place of the barren in this village?"

He held his wife close and helped her head lean on his shoulders as he tried to put her together, boasting to deal with her. She cleared her eyes upon hearing this.

"*Ehe!*" she shouted, that was what I've been wanting and waiting to hear from you at least she will know her place in this village."

They both went inside the hut while she carried the basket along.

Chapter Two

I t was about six o'clock when the two women fought. Ejikeme was on the verandah of his hut splitting firewood.

He wore old shorts and a black singlet that hung loose on his shoulder. Nwanyimma sat on the wooden chair on the front porch of the kitchen, close to her hut. She was pounding an ogbono seed and was about to cook. She sat with her legs in-between the mortar, tied a wrapper that extends from her chest to her legs, wore a sleeveless blouse this time, and tied a black head tie around her head. She pounded the ogbono seeds on the mortar continually, raising her hands up and down, hitting the ogbono seed inside the mortar with the pestle as it made the sound *kpom, kpom,* this sent signals into the air.

Bingo lay close to her with her head placed on top of her front legs, gazing at Nwanyimma as she pounded the ogbono seeds with all the strength she had. Ejikeme placed the first log of the firewood on the chopping block and examined the wood before splitting it. He brought the maul up and down. On hitting it, the wood failed to split on the first swing. He pulled the axe a bit out of the log and continually repeated his swing into the wood to split them. Soon enough, he was about to chop the last wood when he heard his brother's voice, roaring like chariot wheels on the hut's entrance. She felt as though she was electrocuted; her brain felt burned, her mouth hung open, and stared blankly at Mazi Ikeobi. Her wandering eye gave her a perpetually distracted look as if only her body was present.

"*O gini*?" Ejikeme shouted as he bent to drop the axe.

When Mazi Ikeobi got closer, the fire in his eyes could cook jollof rice, and the rage that boiled through his body was beyond control.

"*Nna anyi*, noo!" she said as she stood to greet Mazi Ikeobi.

Infuriated, he shouted, "Who's your Nna? Don't you know the difference between that witch father of yours from Akpuato and me, Mazi Ikeobi? Eze *adighi epempe* one of Amagwu-Nze?"

Mazi Ikeobi always saw himself as the best and was wearing a ripped, torn, short which suggested a man with no earthly cause for pride. Yet, he likened himself to the best.

Still surprised at the whole ordeal, Ejikeme tried to defend his wife and shouted at his older brother,

"Not in this house! Not this time!" As he pointed his finger at Mazi Ikeobi.

Mazi Ikeobi angrily said to him; "I won't blame you because my only brother is under a spell."

"It is okay Nn*a anyi*, please, what's the problem that we (can't or can?) settle amicably?" She asked in a calm, unhurried voice.

This time, anger crept into Mazi Ikeobi's voice which made him shout at her uncontrollably.

"*Taa*! *Kpuchie onu*, do you think I'm your husband that you've put under a spell? *Abu m atakata agboo,* stop your deceptive act *biko*," he said.

Ejikeme was befuddled by the whole drama. He told his brother to take it easy and tell him what the problem is.

"Oh!" Ikeobi shouted, "So she didn't tell you? How will she know the recompense of her actions?"

Ejikeme, thrown in a state of confusion asked; "*Nkem*! Can you tell me what the problem is? Tell me, what exactly is he talking about?"

Nwanyimma was about to speak when Mazi Ikeobi interrupted her.

"Ejikeme," he called. Ejike looked at him as he talked. "You know what an elder sat down and saw? That even a child who climbed an iroko tree will not see..." He continued as he points his light-skinned finger at Nwanyimma, "I warned you as your only brother from marrying from Akpuato, but you gave me a deaf ear, nevertheless, this is not the time for plenty talks. This thing you call your wife," before he could finish speaking, Ejike shouted at him never to refer to his wife as a thing again. Ikeobi ignored him, shook his head in surprise, and continued with what he was about to say before he interrupted him, "I'm only here to tell you that your wife will face the whole villagers in some days now to tell us what gave her the impetus to fight my *acharaugo* with four children. If a snake bites the tortoise, he breaks off his mouth," he added. "You and I know too well that it's against the tradition of this community for a barren woman to fight a mother with child," he also said.

Ejikeme with his mouth opened to his jaw stood in surprise, he looked at his wife and asked her,

"*Nkem*, I don't know you for fighting, what would've led you into fighting her?" She was about to talk when Ikeobi said, "I think I'll leave you both to talk but see you soon at the Igwe's palace to face your repercussions. Maybe, that time my brother will be free from your charm and he'll realize that you've done more harm than good." He turned and started leaving but Ejikeme tried to stop him pleading the matter shouldn't be solved under the king's custody since it is a family issue.

"Is it not better to solve it at home than to take it to the public?" he said softly.

Ejikeme became afraid knowing he was in dread danger if the matter is allowed to be decided by the king. The village has unworthy elders that parade around, always looking for trouble and will make things difficult. "It's not new to know this," Ejikeme spoke. The hairs on his brother's head were all facing toward the front because he was not ready to listen to his brother. Nwanyimma was mute, befuddled, she crossed her arms as though the weather was cold. When Mazi Ikeobi left without uttering a word, Ejikeme walked to his wife, on a low tone and look of worry on his face he asked,

"*Nkem*, but you didn't tell me that something happened between you and mama Ifenyinwa? I know you too well, what could have caused the fight?"

Nwanyimma told him everything that happened; her husband drew her closer and told her that nothing will happen, promising her that he'll be there to protect her. Tears like water kept rolling down her eyes as her husband kept putting her together, and cleaning them with his hand. They both went inside the hut.

Ikeobi got home that evening, Akachi and Nnedi were at the verandah of the hut playing. Akachi was the third child of Mazi Ikeobi is four years old while his sister Nnedi was just two.

Akachi wore an old short with several holes at the buttocks; other children always say that it's where diffusion took place. Nnedi the last child of Mazi wore a pant that looked like the last time it was washed was when their grandmother was getting married. Seeing their father, they got up immediately and dropped the porridge sand they were cooking and ran on their heels as they shouted "*Nna! Nna! Nna!*" they got to him, and embraced him by the sides while Mazi Ikeobi carried Nnedi, "*Kedu?*" he asked the children.

"*O di mma*," they both chorused.

"Akachi, where's your mother?" he inquired.

"Mama is in the kitchen," Akachi answered.

The small kitchen sited at the back of the hut had planks on the wall for placing pots and plates. Ifenyinwa the first child of Mazi Ikeobi was with her mother in the kitchen while Chioye was with the other children playing in the village playground.

He sat down on a bench at the verandah of the hut and told Akachi to go and tell the mother that he was back. Akachi ran and told his mother that their father is back. On hearing this, mama Ifi could not wait to run on her heels because she has been eager to hear the latest development.

"*Nna anyi noo*," she greeted.

"*Kedu Nkem?*" Ikeobi asked.

"*Odimma*," she said as she squatted to sit beside her husband.

Mazi Ikeobi moved a little so his wife can sit. When she sat down, Mazi told her how everything went and later told her, "I'm going to see the elders tomorrow, so we will discuss how to make her the defaulter."

"Thank you, my husband, at least you need to teach her a lesson or even send her out of this village before she ruins the life of your only brother," she smiled and hugged her husband.

"I can do anything for my wife. Who does she think she is? A common barren woman, she's cursed by the gods." They both laughed as they talk ill of Nwanyimma.

She got up, retied her wrapper, and said to her husband, "*Nna anyi* let me go and finish the delicious *achi* soup with *anu nchi* I was preparing for you so that you can eat since you fought more than the mightier."

"Ha, ha, ha," he smiled; "It's like you are aware of the hallowed out feeling in my belly. Please do so quickly before the worms in my stomach start eating my intestines," he said as he smiled continually.

"*Oo Nna anyi*," she replied. "*Nne mama ya*" she petted Nnedi, keep your father busy let me get back to the kitchen," she said touching her on the lower jaw and leaving for the kitchen.

It was about five in the evening, the day after Mazi Ikeobi went to Ejike's hut. He was in the village bar drinking with the other four elders. The bar was the only known bar in the community owned by Nwanyi Ukwunnu. Obiageli is her name but is colloquially called Nwanyi Ukwunnu by the villagers because of her big buttocks. Nwanyi Ukwunnu was still unmarried because people believed that marrying a woman as fat as her was a terrible mistake. She was considered a lazy woman since the village was known for farming which requires being energetic and not fat. All the suitors that came to marry her from the neighboring villages went back to quarrel with the people that recommended her. She's used to her spinster life. She knew that nobody will come knocking for her hand in marriage except some of the village's corrupt chiefs who seek friendship. She's a beautiful woman in her forties. She was in the bar serving her customers with Ndidiamaka, her niece who always comes by in the evening to help her. The four elders that sat with Mazi Ikeobi were: Mazi Okonkwo who is skinny, dark, and of average height; Elder Nweke who is cunning with grey hair that people believed was an ancestral gift, short and of average body build; Chinweokwu who is referred as Akpalaokwu because of his use of deep words and idioms in his speech, he is light-skinned, and of average body build, with a beard that covered his upper and lower jaw; and Mazi Ikeokwu who had little hair on his lower jaw that gave him the look of a goat, the children would run away from him as he was ridiculed for resembling this animal. They have all gathered to conspire and make his brother's wife Nwanyimma the defaulter. They sat in a round table manner under the big *gmelina* tree on the west side of the local bar. They all wore their *isiagu* (lion head).

Mazi Ikeobi motioned at Nwanyi Ukwunnu, signaling her to come. She ran as her buttocks knocked at each other producing the sound pom, pom! The elders couldn't help themselves from gossiping about her steps as her buttocks moved. She got to the elders, squatting to greet them.

"Good evening my elders," she greeted with her leg bent and hand on her lap.

"*Ehe*," the elders replied. "*Kedukwanu*?" they asked her.

"*O di mma*," she replied.

Without hesitation, Mazi Ikeobi asked the elders to tell her what they need. They asked for their different brands. Nwanyi Ukwunnu as she's called ran in and brought bottles of palm wine for the elders which she placed on a tray pan, and served them pepper soup made of *anu nchi* as they requested. They started drinking and taking the pepper soup as they talk.

"*Ewo*!" Chinweokwu shouted, "So Ukwunnu can make this delicious pepper soup?"

"The day I went to my maternal home, I ate the woman's pepper soup, she presumed it to be the best, but it seem not to see the best compared to Ukwunnu's own," Nweke said as he took the meat from the pepper soup plate trying to put it in his mouth.

After several minutes of discussion, Ikeobi cleared his throat in wholesome nature, looked at the elders, nodded with his head, and told them why he had sent for them. They all nodded their heads in unison and agreed to make Nwanyimma the defaulter. They planned how it is going to happen. First, they have to buy the minds of the two maidens that separated them the day they fought so that they'll lie and say that they saw Nwanyimma insult, beat, and injure mama Ifi. Mazi Okonkwo cut in, he cleared his throat, took a brief breath, and said,

"Ehem," he shouted. "My daughter Ekemma told me how they separated your wife and Nwanyimma that day."

"This means the case was settled since it was Okonkwo's daughter. We will then plan to meet the king," Mazi Nweke replied.

"Who is the second maiden?" Chinweokwu asked.

"Adaobi, the daughter of the famous old warrior, Agumba," Nweke replied.

"Okwuna na uka," Ikeokwu said." Do you think that Agumba will agree to this? That man carries his shoulder as if he's *killi wills Nwachukwu*," he included.

"That longer throat? With a bottle of palm wine and good pepper soup from Ukwunnu he'll succumb to everything we say," Okonkwo said softly.

"That means the case is settled. We'll plan on how to meet the king so that everything will be in order," Elder Nweke suggested.

They all agreed to nominate Mazi Nweke and Okonkwo to go with Mazi Ikeobi to the king's palace the following day. So that the wicked witch will leave their village and their brother will be freed, they all said. Mazi Ikeobi thanked them for honoring his invitation and promised to do more after everything is in order. He motioned to Nwanyi Ukwunnu again, signaling her to come. She ran to answer the elders' call. Mazi Ikeobi brought a huge amount of Nigerian *Naira* full of five, ten, and twenty-dollar bills (dollar or naira?) and paid her. She thanked the elders and they all stood up and left.

Three days later, the elders have gone to the Igwe to bribe him into falsehood. At about six O'clock in the evening, the Igwe ordered one of the elders to tell the village town crier to tell everybody to gather at the Igwe's palace exactly at eight O'clock in the morning. The town crier followed the king's instruction.

The day they were supposed to go to the Igwe's palace fell on Eke Day. It is a generational tradition for the villagers to stay at home on this holiday. This is respected by every family since the wrath of the gods would befall those who do not follow.

It was about seven-thirty when all legs were going to the Igwe's palace; young and old, women and men, maidens and boys alike. The maidens dressed neatly, especially those who have attained the age of marriage because they thought luck might befall them. Many of them wore short wrappers and all wore shining beads. The women with babies carried them on their backs with a strip of clothing binding the two with a knot at the chest. No sooner than later, they all arrived at the Igwe's palace. The king had a good number of robust guards and beautiful maidens that served there. Guards of the palace stood dutifully, directing the villagers on where to sit. They sat on the verandah of the good-looking hut painted with local drawings on its walls. These images depicted a king with high authority. The elders sat on the seat prepared for them behind the king's chair, while Nwanyimma and her husband sat on the third row of the bench on the east side of the palace. The villagers sat and talked amongst themselves while they waited for the king's arrival. The atmosphere frowned like they knew the truth was to be hidden. The noise that came from their discussion echoed in the air. It was already eight-twenty in the morning when they saw the Igwe walking majestically with his two wives. The palace guards walked alongside them with glittering machetes. The king is tall, huge, and brown. A handsome man with a befitting simile. No wonder AmagwuNze was taken to be the land of handsome kings as it has always been in the village's history. On seeing him, the villagers stood echoing, "*Igwe! Igwe! Igwe!*"

The Igwe got to his seat, waved at his subjects, smiled, took a brief look at them, and sat on his throne. The throne was decorated with a chieftaincy wrapper that has a picture of a lion's head. The two elegant wives also sat down with beaming smiles on their faces. The second wife sat closer to Igwe because she bore two male children for the king. The first wife also had two female children, but the worth of a child born in Amagwu-Nze was still measured by the presence or absence of a male organ. The people upheld tranquility. The king thanked them for honoring his invitation and called on the Onowu to introduce the people to why they had gathered at the palace. The Onowu, chief Onwudibe dressed in his traditional outfit, wearing an *isiagu* top that resembled the African Dashiki, patterned with a lion's head embroidered all over. He wore it with black trousers and had a title holder's hat on his round head. Chief Onwudibe is a good-looking man in his early fifties. He was a powerful orator and was always chosen to speak on such occasions. He stood up to greet the king, nodding with his head, moved his hand over his chieftaincy hat to adjust it. He stood in the midst of them and bellowed four times "*Cha! Cha! Cha! Cha! Ndi be anyi kwenu!*" he displayed staggering.

"*Iyaaaa!*" the villagers echoed.

And on each occasion, he faced a different direction and seemed to push the air with a clenched fist. He then began to speak.

"Some already know why we gather here while the majority of us are yet to know. Our fathers said the frog does not run in the daytime in vain, it's either he's after something or something is after him." He looked at the elders, then looked around and continues; "The Igwe", he looked at the king, "Has invited us here to listen and hear how two women in our village fought like a cat and a dog some days ago. I beg us to listen as the king passes his fair judgment. Thank you," he said and walked to his seat, and sat down.

The Igwe thanked him and ordered his guards to bring the two women to the middle. The robust-looking guards motioned to the women to come forward and stand before the villagers to face their judgment. The Igwe stood up as he wanted to talk to his subjects, cleared his throat in wholesome nature *ku, ku, ku*, waited, and continued; "The Good people of Amagwu-Nze," he called.

"*Igwe ee!*" the villagers echoed.

"I think it's time for the women standing before us to tell us why they decided to fight like children on their way to the farm. First, they wronged the gods of harvest that day, isn't it?" The Igwe asked.

"It is *ooo!*" the people answered in unison with a murmur of suppressed anger.

The Igwe thanked them, tucked his gown as he bent to sit down, then motioned to the Onowu Chief Onwudibe to continue. The chief stood up; beckoned with his head the second time, and thanked the Igwe.

"Mama Ifenyinwa," Onwudibe called.

"*Eeh nna anyi,*" she answered.

"Please can you tell the people what happened that day?" Onwudibe said.

Mama Ifi looked at the Igwe, bowed down as she echoed continually,

"*Igwe! Igwe!*" she turned to the villagers, "*Ndewonu*, people of Amagwu-Nze," she greeted.

"*Ndewo*," the villagers replied.

She put her hands on her back, and continued, "Everybody here knows that I'm a peaceful woman who never looked for anybody's trouble. That fateful day, I was going to the farm when suddenly I came across this woman," pointing her finger at Nwanyimma; "Even her dog will bear me witness." She continued as she shed crocodile tears, "I passed when she stopped and pushed me, telling me that I gave deaf ears to her greetings. Knowing fully well that it's against the law of our village to fight on the day we're going to the farm, I was about to leave when she pushed and slapped me. Not only that, she even called me all sorts of names like a barbaric, and a witch. What annoyed me the most was when she overpowered me, throwing me on the ground and giving me a heavy beating. I thank the gods for the two maidens who ran to my rescue," she said as she continued wiping out tears from her eyes. "When I got up, I was bruised and wounded," she showed the villagers where she was injured.

"Abomination! *Aru!*" the villagers shouted uniformly, "*Tufiak-wa!*" THEY also cursed.

"I think I'm done, thank you Igwe and the elders of our land."

Onwudibe stood up again, bowed as he greeted the Igwe, and turned to the villagers, I call for mama Ifi to step down while he told Nwanyimma to tell them any lie mama Ifi said. Ejikeme's buttocks could no longer relax on the bench he sat on, his temper was flaring as he kept tossing restlessly on the bench, but he took hold of himself. Nwanyimma thanked the Igwe and the villagers and told her side of the story but the Igwe stood up to end the judgment. Nwanyimma's heart plunged to her STOMACH as she already knew the conclusion will not be fair to her due to her condition. She held her breath in fear.

The Igwe continued, "My people we already know from the time of our forefathers that we're not allowed to fight on the farm day, it's clear the defaulters will bear every fault. It's obvious that Nwanyimma has not shown any remorse. We heard from the maidens that separated them, I think they were explicative enough by telling us how Nwanyimma cursed, pushed, and injured her fellow woman." He said and allowed a murmur of suppressed anger to sweep the crowd.

"*Aru!*" the unjust elders shouted.

The Igwe continued,

"Nevertheless, since the birth of our culture, we know that a barren woman shall not fight a woman with a child because our ancestors believed they are cursed. Having considered all this, I hereby declare Nwanyimma guilty."

"What!" Ejikeme shouted as he got up quickly from the bench. His eyes boiled with rage and it showed all over his body. The depth of his pain could not be expressed in words. Assuming he can kill the Igwe and the elders with his eyes; he'd do it immediately without sparing anybody's life, including his brother and his wife. He managed to take a hold of himself, so he won't make things worse or create a scene. The Igwe was still speaking when Nwanyimma started begging that she and mama Ifi will settle their issues amicably when they get home. Mama Ifi bluntly refused to say that Igwe's judgment will be final. The Igwe cleared his throat and continued, "Having caused this anxiety to your fellow woman knowing your position in Amagwu, I now declare that you are exiled from Amagwu for three years and you cannot be near the village until the punishment lapses."

Nwanyimma trapped in a dark reality she did not believe, got to her knees, and pleaded that her ban be lifted; that she'll never fight in Amagwu again, she cried and cried but the Igwe left while the elders walked away in jubilation, including Mazi Ikeobi and wife. Ejikeme stood mouth wide open as he gazed in awed, silence. His wife lay on the floor crying. The villagers had all taken their different routes except mama Ezekwesiri, a melancholy woman in the era who believed that men and women are equal. She never supported the tradition of Amagwu people imposing so many negative responsibilities on barren women. She spent fifteen years with her late husband before the gods blessed them with a child. She has been in Nwanyimma's shoes and knows how it pains. She puckered her lips and sank deep in thought, she later decided to walk up to Nwanyimma and talk to her. She stood up, retied her wrapper, and walked to where Mma lay helplessly.

"It is okay!" she said with a voice that sounded like a man's as she tucked her wrapper trying to squat down tapping Mma on the shoulder. She told her how they humiliated her because of the same barren condition.

She raised her head trying to know the person who was encouraging her when she has been abandoned by all. This time, her husband walked up to them and stood mute as he looked at his wife while mama Ezekwesiri talked to her. At first, Nwanyimma thought it was a man talking to her because she had never met mama Ezekwesiri. She has been in her maternal home ever since her husband died.

"Do you mean you have gone through this ordeal before?" Nwanyimma asked as she sobbed.

"Yes!" Mama Ezekwesiri answered, "I received a lot of insults from the people of Amagwu. They believed that I'm a man wearing the form of a woman because of my voice."

"Thank the gods for you," she said softly. "I wish the gods will answer my prayers even if it's for a female child to prove to the people that I'm not what they think I'm," she said sadly.

"Patient my dear, who are we to question the gods in their makings?" Mama Eze softly said. "The gods will see you through but if I may advise, I want you to leave this village because they are heartless, after that three years they ordered you, to come back but believe me "the gods are wise," she included.

Ejikeme squatted, held his wife, helped her to stand, shouldered her, and told her to stop crying; that things will get back to normal someday. He thanked Mama Ezekwesiri, as they left the Igwe's palace.

Chapter Three

Two days after the Igwe declared Nwanyimma guilty; she was in her hut packing her clothes as she cried.

Nwanyimma stood on the floor of the mud house packing her clothes in her rectangular box. Bingo lay there with two hind feet on the front and pricked ears as she watched for a moment and then yawned. Ejikeme was not at the house when his wife was packing. He had gone to his friend's house to plead for him to work on his farm on Orie day because the field is too big for one man to till. Nwanyimma had cried out her eyes since that day. Her eyes were swollen and turned red like she's been smoking cigarettes for a couple of weeks.

She was still packing when suddenly Bingo started barking, "Woof! Woof! Woof!". Bingo stood up from where she lay barking ferociously, moving towards mama Ezekwesiri who was coming through the narrow entrance of the hut.

"Bingo! Bingo!" Mma called as she came out of the hut with her blouse, which she mistakenly took. Bingo on hearing her voice started going back. When mama Ezekwesiri got close, they embraced themselves warmly and exchange greetings. Mama Ezekwesiri looked at her eyes and discovered that she has been crying out her eyes. She advised her that it will one day get back to normal.

"How long?" she asked, "Ages? Century? In the grave?" she included.

"Soon!" mama Ezekwesiri replied, "let us go inside I've many things to gist you."

They both went in. Seeing her box already packed,

"Don't you think the Igwe may reverse the statement he made and have a change of heart?" she said as she sat on the wooden chair beside the bed. "It is high time we stood our ground; it is time barren women shouldn't be ostracized."

"What do you want us to do now?" Nwanyimma asked softly. "Hold the bull by the horn?" She nodded in disagreement and continued. "I'm now waiting for the gods to look at my weeping face and shut that mouth that's jabbering if the good thing will ever come from Akpuato."

"*Amii ooo*! The gods shall shut the whining mouths and their groundless rumor will stop."

Nwanyimma was grateful to have somebody in AmagwuNze who put a smile on her weeping face again. She saw awareness and altruism bestowed upon her with these small acts of kindness shown. She became excited that at least she was not dejected by everybody, and thanked her for being with her when she thought she was alone. Mama Ezekwesiri reminded her that she had been in her plight. Perhaps she wouldn't sit, keeping her fingers crossed when she knew she can do something even if she won't be able to change it but at least, "I'm happy that you can smile again," she added. "I know the gods will remember you just as they had shown reminiscence to me," she said as she stood up untying and retying her wrapper. "Mma, I'll be on my way, I said it's wise to check on you before you leave for Akpuato," she said.

"Oh! *Ezigbo nwanyi* let me look for something for you," Nwanyimma said as she got up and about to go to the inner hut but mama Ezekwesiri refused to say

"It isn't time for merriment, that time shall come," she added.

She was led outside by Nwanyimma and she started going home as Nwanyimma went in and continued with what she was doing.

In the evening of that same day, Nwanyimma prepared for her journey to Akpuato, her paternal village. It will be the worst nightmare going back to Akpuato since her mother and father is late. The home-owner is Omah, her stepmother. Omah is a woman who is belligerent, callous, and eager to destroy. This is why most women in Akpuato hate her. Her husband loved her more than Nwanyimma's mother because she gave him two hefty boys with who he would hand every-thing over before his death. The culture of not recognizing female children is common to both Akpuato and Amagwu-Nze. She wore an embroidered puffed sleeve blouse and tied a brown wrapper with a head scarf. She carried her small box while Ejikeme wore shorts and an old black polo shirt. He carried the big box on his head. The expression on Ejikeme's face showed that he was deeply sad. He promised heaven and earth to his wife and promised to wait for her to come back. If not for culture, it is obvious Ejikeme would go to Akpuato with his wife to settle. Nwanyimma who's deeply depressed only calmed her husband by telling him the gods shall fight for them. Perhaps, our people will say, "where one falls is where his *chi* pushed him down," but in this case, they have been pushed down by mortals, not their god. They walked as they talked. They got to the border between Akpuato and Amagwu; dropped what they carried, he hugged her tightly, and reassured her that it was well. That evening, it looked as if the sky was about to weep. It let out lightning and thunder. He told his wife to start going to avoid being drenched in the rain. He stood mute while his wife carried her boxes and continued turning to look at her husband as they wave at one another to say goodbye. For an hour, Ejikeme stood saying goodbye while the wife walked slowly. When he could no longer see his wife because she has gone far beyond his sight, he walked home. At night, Ejikeme could not sleep as he tossed restlessly on the bed as though he was having a terrible nightmare. He lay on the bed as he gazed at the thatched roof, though he couldn't see anything because the room was dark since he turned off the lantern while trying to sleep. He was on his bed as the wind roared and the cold rain was pouring. Ejikeme thought of his wife throughout the cold night.

Two weeks after Nwanyimma left for her paternal village, Ejikeme was getting ready to go to the farm when his brother came in with his problem of marrying another wife. He's still inside the hut getting ready, he took his singlet and hung it on a nail on the mud wall. He bent when he got to the mouth of the door since he was about a foot taller than the door. When he came out, he saw Mazi Ikeobi marching to his hut, though still at the hut entrance. Ejikeme held the door by the handle and locked it. Mazi Ikeobi who was not too far from his brother started shouting.

"*Nwanne adina mba*!" With a beaming smile on his face as he knocked his walking stick continually on the ground as he walked.

"*O ginikwa na ututu a*?" he answered harshly.

He got close, and saw that his brother was moody, he inquired to know what the problem is.

"What is that brother?" he asked, "Why is your face like mud sand? Is anything the matter?" he included.

Ejikeme cleared his throat *ku, ku, ku,*

"What do you want me to say?" he asked. "Say that everything is well? All is not well," he included.

"Ah!" Ikeobi shouted, "But your brother is always here to help out, okay now tell me, what's your problem?" he inquired.

Ejikeme looked at him, shook his head in surprise, and continued.

"If not that you are my brother, I would've asked you out of my house," he said.

Surprisingly, Ikeobi's mouth opened to his jaw in dismay, he shouted,

"Abomination! Aru! Thank the gods you said if I weren't your brother," he included. "Please brother, our people said the frog does not run in the daytime in vain," Ikeobi added. "I'm only here because I've your interest at heart;" he paused, looked at his brother, and continued. "It is only a mother who loves her child who will beat him with the right hand and draw him closer with the left hand."

Ejikeme was intensely thinking about the farm before he was stopped by his so-called older brother.

"Why don't you hit the nail and stop beating about the bush," Ejikeme said in a harsh voice. "As you can see, I was about to go to the farm before you suddenly appeared from nowhere," he added.

Mazi Ikeobi looked behind his back, looked right and left, but could not see any other person standing there with them.

"Are you talking to me?" he inquired.

"Of course," Ejikeme replied, "What do you want?"

He drew closer and held Ejikeme by the shoulder with his left hand while he held his chieftaincy staff in the right hand.

"Though we share different mothers and the same father, you're more than a brother to me," Ikeobi said.

Ejikeme still stood stunned as he held his face forward in a steady gaze at his brother while he talked.

"My little brother," Mazi Ikeobi continued, "You're a man of integrity, a farmer well-known and respected in AmagwuNze, your fatherland," he paused, and looked at Ejikeme who squeezed his face like an old rumpled cloth, looked at every nook and cranny of the compound, and continued, "Look at all this, the rich barn," pointing at the barn sited behind the hut, "The house, perhaps, all your riches? Who do you want to inherit them? Or you haven't given a thought about this?" He inquired.

This time Ejikeme pushed to ask,

"What do you want me to do? Hold the bull by the horn?" He nodded in disagreement. "*Aru!*" he shouted, "So patient my brother, I'm still looking at the face of the gods of our land."

"Quiet!" Ikeobi shouted angrily, "Quiet Ejike, for how long will you wait for the gods? Consider your age brother; you're not getting any younger," he said.

Ejikeme calmly asked, "So what do you want me to do?"

"*Ehe*! Now you're talking," he said smiling. "Let us now talk *tete-a-tete*. As it stands now brother, I think you only need a young maiden from this village, just one play (*ofu mgba*, he said in the Igbo language) and it will enter," he spoke with his hands as he continued smiling.

Ejikeme annoyed on hearing this, felt like killing his brother with his bare hands, and looked at his brother as rage boiled through his body. The hairs on his head stood in anger while he was blue in the face.

"When you're done marrying, you know the route to your house." He left the house as he held the handle of the hoe which hung on his shoulder with his left hand.

Having stood mute for some minutes, Mazi Ikeobi nodded in disappointment, "Wonders shall never end!" He shouted as he turned to take his leave. "This woman's charm is so strong; I think we need witch-hunters to hunt her before my brother will get free. I must get him to marry another wife. Let me quickly get going because I've to see Omaricha's father so we'll discuss the marriage rite. My brother needs to marry immediately before it gets out of hand," he said as walked fast leaving the compound.

It was on Afo day in Akpuato, and Nwanyimma was getting ready to go to Nneka's shop to learn how to sew clothes. She decided to learn sewing as a livelihood. They are not known for farming because the Akpuato soil is mostly sandy. They always argue that they started cloth making before Amagwu village but the people of Amagwu have never agreed since people from neighboring villages view them as the best. People came from far and near to sew cloth in Amagwu. Though after Amagwu village, Akpuato would be the second in line since it is their main occupation. People that cannot sew usually go to Amagwu and other neighboring villages to work for pay and food.

It was exactly seven-twenty in the morning on Afo day; Nwanyimma wore a blue gown that extended to her legs and tied a red scarf. Omah, her stepmother sat under a mango tree on the verandah of the hut. The compound had two mud houses. It's large and surrounded by bushes a few kilometers away from the huts. She's an old woman in her mid-sixties. In Omah's old age, she's well-known in Akpuato for being a troublemaker, a big nuisance to the family of Nwanyimma when her parents were still alive. She thought she had changed after all those years she had been without seeing her, but nothing was different. Omah sat under the tree looking for trouble saying that she was receiving fresh air. Nwanyimma knew that Omah was only coming for trouble when she got to where she stood.

"Eem, Eem, semistress," she called timidly referring to a seamstress. "*Nne m,*" Nwanyimma answered.

"Taa!" she shouted, "Who is your *Nne*? You and I who's older? Take a good look at me," she turned three- a hundred and sixty degrees as she untied and retied her wrapper swaying her waist, "You know I've given birth to two hefty men that are married and I'm still *a kwa a kwuru*," she included, "You've not removed anything from your body, and you are like this."

"Mama, what did I do to you this early morning?" Nwanyimma asked in a calm voice.

"Ah! So you don't know the worst you've done is to come back to this house after marriage," Omah said. "Your life has been in misery," she added.

Tears streamed down Nwanyimma's eyes this time, she tried to clear the tears with her hand.

"What did I say for you to start shedding those crocodile tears of yours?" She asked. "The history of Akpuato had not recorded a chasing of a woman out of her husband's house because of barrenness and witchcraft, I *ga-abu Ogbenye buru amosu*?" She asked. "I heard from people that it's because of your stubbornness that your husband's people chased you out. If you want to remain in this compound, you must do as I say, if not, you have me to contend with. *Ogu m ga-emeri* (the fight I will win), I'm not asking the gods to help me," she included. Nwanyimma did not utter a word as she said those things.

"You know my two children; their wives and children are living here. It will be wise if you look for another place to stay until the gods need you," she said.

This time Nwanyimma left without saying a word.

"*Amosu*," Omah shouted. "Look at her," she said pointing at Nwanyimma; "*Mtchew!*" She made the sound with her mouth by squeezing and sucking her teeth to show how she disliked her step-daughter. "Like mother like daughter," she added. "You can never live in this house with me. I think you have overstayed your welcome. That reminds me, I heard that Onyeze, the blind is looking for a wife," she said. "This is a perfect wife for him," she said as she walked towards the hut as continued talking. "I'll see him later in the evening to discuss it."

When Nwanyimma got to Afo Akpuato, all other seamstresses and male tailors had already arrived and started with their daily work. Afo Akpuato is a market that opens on only Afo day. People from all over go there to sell and buy. The market is rowdy, both old and young alike were seen selling and buying. In fact, it was as busy as an anthill. The shop where Nwanyimma is learning her dressmaking is found on the east side of the market. It's an open shop built with bamboo trees and thatched on the roof. When she came in, she greeted and went to the chief seamstress Nneka, who was in charge of teaching her. Nneka loved her because she was a fast learner and so down to earth and had already made up her mind that she would become a close friend with her because she believed that she was naturally talented, dedicated, and respectful. She got close to her and sat on a stool in front of the sewing machine with her hands on the machine. Nneka's face radiates with a smile. Nwanyimma bent as she gave her a warm smile and tapped her on the back.

"*Ututuoma Ma!*" Nneka greeted.

"*Kedukwanu?*" she asked as she took a stool beside her to sit down.

"*Odimma!*" Nneka replied, "This one you came late today, hope all is well?" She asked in a low tone as she got the machine ready to sew the next dress she picked from the basket.

"Haa!" she shouted, paused her lips a little, and continued. "*Nnem*, my stepmother has refused to let me drink and keep the cup."

"Ah!" Nneka shouted, "So after all these years you weren't in this village this woman's attitude hasn't changed a little bit towards you?"

She nodded surprisingly. "Wonder shall never end," she said as she bent trying to put a thread on the tiny needle on the sewing machine. "I have always heard from my mother how this same woman maltreated you and your mother when she was alive," Nneka raised her head, looked at Nwanyimma, "Do not relent, the gods are wise in their judgment and they will remember you one day," she included.

"Thank you, my dear," Nwanyimma replied.

"Come closer," Nneka said as she was trying to pass the thread through the tiny needle. "This gown we're going to sew now is a new design. I'd want you to learn it. It has not been in the market, but I learned it when I went to my maternal home in Nsukka."

Nwanyimma took a brief breath of relief, tucked her gown, and sat attentively as Nneka teaches her new style.

It was six in the evening on Afo day; the people that came to the market from the neighboring villages started taking their different routes so the night will not befall them or avoid the rain since it was a rainy season. Nwanyimma was walking home on the narrow path with bushes and low trees left and right. The breeze whispered to the heavens and the sky looked as if it was weeping. She walked quickly so the rain will not beat her. Having walked for about nine poles from the market, she came across Okpalaugo who stood amid a freshly planted maize field, urinating. She's not surprised why Okpalaugo is urinating at the maize field because nobody in his right senses would do such a thing. Okpalaugo is a drunkard though and can talk senses when not drunk. People believed the gods always use them to send messages. Why the gods decided to use Vagabonds like drunkards is still a mystery they're yet to understand.

"Ah!" Nwanyimma shouted in dismay, "Okpalaugo, why are you urinating on that maize field?" She asked.

Okpalaugo zipped up his trouser, drew them to his chest, and held it with rope, staggering around as he points at Nwanyimma.

"Mma! Mma!" he called.

"*O gini*!" Nwanyimma asked.

"Thank the gods that we met here, I came back from my maternal home today and heard that you're in Akpuato. I hurriedly went to your place," he paused as he took the last drop of the alcohol in the bottle; shook it in his mouth, and swallowed it. "Ehem!" he exclaimed, "When I got to your hut, I saw that too-old-to-die stepmother of yours."

Nwanyimma who was in a haste to get home before the rain started inquired to know why he was looking for her.

He smiled, looked at Nwanyimma, and said, "The gods are wise, indeed, you're different from every other woman Mma; I was imagining how you manage to stay with that grumpy and unprincipled Omah and her two troublesome sons and wives. Eem!" he continued "you know I have missed that melon soup you use to cook when you were still in Akpuato before you married," he said smiling.

"Was that why you were looking for me?" she said as she smiled.

He staggered again and continued.

"Not at all Mma, I've heard all that happened, I want to tell you the gods made them that way."

"How do you mean?" she inquired.

"Mma, you will soon understand the gods cannot be confused in their makings. I know that Amagwu has always chimed into the culture, will good ever come from Akpuato?" he smiled as he points continually at her. "Time is coming when the whole world will need a child the gods will give you."

She laughed in doubt this time and told him to stop it, "Nevertheless, I'm already at the menopause stage where I heard that women will not be able to give birth again."

Okpalaugo stammered trying to pronounce menopause.

"Me-ee-no-pause or mee-no-bag or which one it is? I have said my own. You should put the meno in the pause. The gods will give you a child who'd make an incredible discovery," he said.

Suddenly, the rain started dropping,

"*Okpala*," Mma said, "see you some other times," she said oblivious to her environment, and backed him to leave.

Okpalaugo staggered the last time; "I'll be at your hut tomorrow for my *Egusi* soup," he said, checking his bottle for any drop of alcohol left.

The rain became more serious, she ran on her heels.

"Ewo! I'm sun drying my melon seeds which I kept on the roof of my hut oh. It will not occur to anyone to take it in for me?" She ran as possible as her legs could. While Okpalaugo took the other route singing not minding how fast the rain was dropping on him.

Chapter Four

At six in the evening, Ejikeme was in his compound, wearing a short and a singlet, and sat on a wooden chair. He had a melon ball with him, and a machete to cut the melon into half. He was scooping out the seeds as he was whistling. Soon enough, his brother arrived with a maiden walking beside him. She carried a basket which contained her clothes, olden days make up such as *uri, uhie, nzu* and ear rings, carried around her arm as she walked behind Mazi Ikeobi swaying her waist like she was on a beauty contest. Ejikeme saw them coming but the hairs on his head never moved as he was busy scooping the melon because he needed to dry them when the sun comes out. However, it is pertinent to know that during the rainy season, the sun hardly comes out. When they got to where he sat, "*Ndewo Nkem!*" Omaricha greeted as she bent to drop the basket, she carried around her arms.

Ejikeme was still busy scooping the melon.

"Ezinwanne how are you?" Mazi Ikeobi asked.

Omaricha slouched with her hands on her waist while she smiled continually. Ejikeme infuriated, angrily asked his brother,

"What exactly do you want?"

Omaricha's instinct began to tell her that her dreams of marrying Ejikeme would be a dream without end. Mazi Ikeobi cleared his throat in wholesome nature, nodded with his head and said,

"I've decided to put a smile on my only brother's face again, brother," he called," Look at this damsel," pointing at Omaricha,

"Show him what you got."

Omaricha turned half round, shook her buttocks like a dog that was wagging its tail to welcome her owner.

"*Nwata na mma,* a buxom waist that makes her man kill a goat for her when he looks at it," Mazi Ikeobi adorned her smiling, "I've paid for her bride price brother and she's now legally your wife. This time next year, I want us here again to dine and thank the gods for a cry of a baby heard."

Ejikeme did not say a word; he kept on scooping the melon as his temper was flaring as he squeezed his face.

"Omaricha," Mazi called, "As you can see, your husband is still in endless stupefaction, unaware that I'm going to come with surprises," he included. "I want you to take your things inside while I leave, cook for your husband and remember to respect him," Ikeobi said.

"Yes, *Nna anyi,*" Omaricha said smiling.

She squatted, carried her basket and was about to go inside the hut when suddenly Ejikeme broke the awed silence.

"You bitch!" Ejikeme furiously shouted as he quickly rose from the wooden chair. "Where do you think you're going?"

With his mouth opened to his jaw a surprised Mazi Ikeobi shouted, "What? Do you call this elegant maiden a bitch?" He nodded his head in dismay. "I do not blame you. You are under a spell, but I bet you, by the time you eat a food prepared by her, you'll be free. Our fathers say that it takes a woman to spoil the charm prepared by another woman for her husband, *biko*, go inside," he ordered.

As rage boiled through Ejike's body, his eyes turned red immediately, anger crept into his voice.

"Please take this ingrate to your house and make her your second wife since you already paid for her bride price, I'm okay with my wife."

"You're such a disappointment," Mazi shouted angrily. "When will you learn to appreciate an act of kindness shown to you?" he asked.

"Kindness you call this?" Ejikeme asked.

"Yes! Kindness," he replied angrily.

"Thank you, brother, but take this out of my house," he said pointing at Omaricha.

He took the melon he scooped which was on a tray pan, his chair, and machete and hurriedly went inside.

"He doesn't love *me Nna anyi*?" Omaricha asked with a calm voice as she shuddered in fear.

"Don't worry my daughter; he'll learn to love you," he assured her.

"For how long N*na anyi*?" **she** asked, "I can feel the anger in his **eye;** he's still deeply in love with Mma. Please N*na anyi* I'm not even interested any more, let me wait for my own husband, a man who'll come to my father's house and pay my bride price," she said as she left quickly.

"Wait! Wait!" Mazi shouted as he ran after her. Our elders say, "the stubborn fowl hears in soup pot," he said to his brother.

It was Eke day in Akpuato; the people have been expecting rain. For three days, there had been no rain. Though their soil is not good enough for planting, they still managed to plant each year through the high rainfall. Nneka decided to pay a visit to Nwanyimma since they only go to market on Afo day. She dressed, wore her gown and tied a blue scarf. Nneka always looked good enough to attract suitors since she was already ripe for marriage, but no man had come to ask if the market is for sale. She locked the wooden door, hid the key on the hut's lower roof. They usually keep it there any time they go out if nobody is around, so anybody that comes home first collects it and gets in the house. She walked about ten steps when suddenly she remembered that she forgot something outside, came back and went to the lower roof of the hut, brought the African salad down from the lower roof, collected the key from the roof, unlocked the hut, kept it inside, locked the door again, and kept the key and left.

When she got to Nwanyimma's hut, Nwanyimma sat under a *gmelina* tree on the verandah of their hut separating chaffs from the adani rice and enjoying the garden egg her husband brought her. The air of authority she had was palpable. Bingo lay close to her. She walked to where Nwanyimma sat.

"*Daalu kwa,*" she greeted.

"Ah! Nneka, why this one unannounced visit you paid me? Hope I'm safe?" she asked smiling.

"You are much safe my sister," she said with a smiling face.

"Thank the gods," she replied as she adjusted and dusted the chair for Nneka to sit beside her.

She sat down, and helped her remove the chaffs from the rice grain. Nwanyimma took a lasting gaze at her.

"Hum!" she exclaimed. "The way you are looking at me, I hope all is well?" she asked.

"*Nne idi* okay! You're beautiful," Nwanyimma adorned her.

"*Umuokorobia Akpuato ha ana-ahukwa uzo?*" she asked in the Igbo language.

"Ah! You're flattering me."

"*Nne wepugodu* that flatter," Mma snapped, how I wish I've a male sibling.

"What'll happen if you do?" Nneka inquired.

"You know *na*, this charming beauty ought to be in this compound now," she said smiling.

"My dear, I'm even beginning to worry because my mother is already disturbing me. She always makes me feel jealous each time my younger sister comes to our house with her two kids," Nneka said with an expression of worry on her face.

"*Eya*!" Nwanyimma shouted, I understand your plight my sister, but we cannot take the bull by the horn. Nevertheless, our people said the breadfruit will fall when the time is due (*Ukwa ruo oge ya*)," she spoke encouragingly. "You're still young and, believe me, suitors are on their way," she included.

"Suitors? People gossiped that my small body physique is confusing. You and I know that they're only saying the truth," said Nneka, I'm not getting any younger. Do you know that we are agemates?" she asked.

"Nneka my sister somebody unmarried is better than me," she said angrily, "Nneka am I not supposed to be in my husband's house?" Nwanyimma asked.

She held the garden egg with her teeth and could not chew, because she was deeply touched by what Mma said, she waited for some minutes and continued chewing.

"Mma my dear, the gods will remember you; the gods will shut the mouths that chimed if something good will ever come from you," she said calmly. "*Ehe*! That reminds me," Nneka snapped, "Heard that your husband was here to see you the day before yesterday?"

Nwanyimma nodded in affirmation and said, "He brought this garden egg."

"*Ezigbo mmadu*," said Nneka. "He's such a caring husband, that's the kind of man my heart wishes and seeks for," she included.

"My dear, Ejikeme my husband, is so caring," said Nwanyimma. "Least I forget, do you know Nwude was here with his people yesterday," she said.

Nneka ran in thought as she repeatedly said "Nwude, Nwude, which of the Nwude?" she inquired.

"How many Nwude do you know?"

"Nwude the blind?" Nneka caught in.

"Yes of course," Nwanyimma replied.

"Ah! What for? I mean for what reason?" **she** quickly asked.

"He came to take me home," she said smiling.

"How? Why? I mean for what reason?" Nneka desperately asked in surprise.

"My dear it's my stepmother, she collected bride price from people for my hand in marriage."

"Abomination!" she shouted as she jumped from her seat.

"That your stepmother is biting more than she can chew, what did you do then?" Nneka asked.

"My dear, I told them that I'm a married woman and will soon be going back to my husband."

"Oh!" She exclaimed, "Trouble do not know road, how I wish I was the one, that your stepmother should've married Nwude yesterday," Nneka said angrily as she boiled in rage. "Nne m, let me tell you, I'm looking for a husband but not Nwude's type, *tufiakwa*!" she spitted out. "It is high time you told the troublesome woman it's enough my friend."

"My dear, I only have six months to stay in this village, I'll go back to my husband soon. "I think I need to learn how to avoid them so to not pick offenses," she said calmly.

"Oh!" Nneka shouted as she sat back, "My softhearted friend. They should thank their gods that Neky (as she's fondly called by friends) is not the one. *Maka na oburu m,* I'll put fire in this compound, *nne,* I respect you more. That reminds **me;** you said you'll be going back in six months?"

"Yes my dear!" Nwanyimma answered.

"Oh! Thank the gods. I'm so happy for you my friend," Nneka said.

"Thank you, my sister," replied Nwanyimma.

"I'm going to miss you and this laughter I admire always," she said as she gazed at Nwanyimma.

"Six months is such a longtime, remember," Nwanyimma said.

"My dear, time flies *o*! Before you know, the six month is here."

"Amagwu is not far from Akpuato, so we'll always see," Nwanyimma assured her.

"*Ee*! That's how you'll say it now but once you go to Amagwu, you'll not remember the good times we had together here in your fatherland," she calmly said.

"Ha, ha, ha! My dear I'll always come by because as soon as I go back to Amagwu, I'll start my own sewing business with all the new styles you taught me. I'll also be coming for new styles," she said smiling.

"Really," inquired Nneka."

"Yes of course," Mma said.

She embraced Nwanyimma as tears of joy trickled down her cheeks.

"My dear, I pray the gods will give you a child that will put a smile on your face when you get to Amagwu." "*Amin o*!" Nwanyimma replied.

Nneka stood, collected one of the garden eggs left on that wooden plate, and took a bite of it.

"I'll be on my way, so that I'll help my mother prepare the breadfruit she wants to take to the market tomorrow."

Nwanyimma stood up, kept the tray of rice on the chair and saw her off.

* * *

Three months later, three men from United States of America Nicolas Lupe, Bryan Wiggins and Walter Eric lost their way on a journey to another country. Eventually, they saw themselves wandering in the land of Amagwu. Nicolas Lupe is a medical doctor by profession, a reproductive endocrinologist, who studied medicine in a renowned school; Stanford University, in California. He later got an award of discovering the drug for treating infertility in women and he's a lecturer in the department of Endocrinology. Bryan Wiggins was a graduate student from the University of Salfold. He always peaked interest on combating infertility for women. He met with Dr. Nicolas Lupe at a conference in Los Angeles when they both discovered that they have the same interest at heart. Walter Eric was an undergraduate student in Stanford University. He is an African and an indigent of Igbo. He is from Aguleri in Anambra State. Walter was sold during the period of slave trade because he was very lazy and stubborn. His *chi* smiled at him when Adolf Michael his master peak a special interest on him. Though he was lazy but smart and intelligent. He lived in Ghana for some years with his master before they travelled back to the USA. He was too young then to remember the road to Ghana. Perhaps, it was almost fifteen years they left Ghana. Nicolas and Bryan brought him to act as an interpreter since he speaks and understands Ghana language. They decided to journey to African countries. Meanwhile, they didn't know the continent that much. They were to go to Ghana and to a case study on infertility in women when their fate found themselves wandering in Amagwu.

At ten twenty- five in the morning on Eke day, the people of Amagwu are usually at home. Nicolas, Wiggins and Walter abandoned their car because there were no roads for the car to take. They have trekked for days and became weary. Luckily for them, they saw a path that had human footprints. They became happy because they believed they must be close to settlements. They kept walking toward the bosky narrow road of Amagwu as they talk. Wiggins kept taking pictures and writing in his notebook. He told Nicolas that he would use Africa in his story when they get back home, and he'll include every picture that he'll take on the course of their hectic journey.

"Ah! Africa has so many untapped resources," Nicolas surprisingly said.

"Honestly they do," Wiggins snapped.

"I've read the history of Africa and learned that they're blessed by nature sir," he said as he bent low to take a picture of a tree that looked like a human being. "One would make an incredible discovery in Africa."

"Yea!" Nicolas shouted, "I doubt they'll give us listening ears because they are still unaware about the existence of what we're bringing to them," Nicolas said.

"Our instinct will help us; they're uneducated, uncivilized and antiquated," Nicolas added.

Walter was a student of Nicolas and he talked less with them. He only affirmed to what they say by nodding of head and smiling.

Having walked for some minutes, they saw two maidens that were not far from them coming in the same direction. The two maidens were the birds of a feather Ekemma and Adaobi. They tied short wrappers above their chest. **And tied** a same colour of wrapper on chest, knotted firmly at the back. They were both talking as they walked. When they got a bit closer to Nicolas, Bryan, **Walter,** they both turned with the speed of light as they shouted, "*Chim o!*"

Running down the narrow bosky road, wind rifled their wrappers and dried out their sapphire dark eyes. Nicolas and Bryan became confused why the maidens were running from them. They were happy to have seen human beings after five days walking from where their car got spoilt. The maidens were still running while they ran past Chinweokwu and Nweke who were both coming from the front talking. The elders stopped to know why the maidens ran like that. When they stopped, they panted heavily.

"Young maidens, what is after you? Why are you both scaring the whole village?" inquired Chinweokwu.

"*Hu*! *Hu*! *Hu*!" **the** maidens panted unable to speak. They were still trying to know what was after the maidens when Bryan, Nicolas and Walter came close. The maidens trapped by heavy panting kept pointing at them as they approached. Suddenly, the elders turned and saw them. They ran as fast as their legs could carry them. Nweke ran faster compared to Chinweokwu who was at the back shouting for Nweke to wait for him.

"*O kwanu ndi muo*!" Nweke kept shouting as he ran.

They got to the village square, they didn't see anyone. The elders alerted them to run for their lives. Nweke ran to the palace and told the king what he had seen. The Igwe ordered four of his robust guards, armed them with weapons to go and know what the elder was talking about. He ordered them

"Ghost or not, whatever it is, bring them to the palace alive." The four guards left on Igwe's command. When they saw **them**, they brought out their sword from the machete cover, raised it as they approach them. Nicolas and Bryan shuddered in fear, and halt in fear. Walter was less afraid because he knew he would have been that naïve if he were in the village. When the guards got close to them. One of the guards squatted, took sand and poured it on them. They were then taken to the palace. They got to the palace, the king was afraid of them for his lips lack descriptions for both. He ordered them thrown in a dungeon until the next Eke day. "They will appear before the villagers, so they tell us who or what they are and why they have decided to defile our community." They followed the Igwe's instruction, and took Nicolas, Bryan and Walter to the dungeon cage. The king ordered the town crier that same day to send a message to the people. Tell them to gather in Igwe's palace the next two market days, being that it was an Eke market day, the matter that needed to be attending to urgently.

It's six-twenty that evening, the villagers started to return from their daily works. Some balanced a basket on their head with a simple length of cloth shaped into a ring. Young maidens coming back from the stream carried brimming water pails balanced on their head. Women carried babies on their backs with strip of cloths that bind them with knot at chest. Elders, wives and children were coming back from their farm. The village road was busy like the anthill that evening.

"*Gum*! *Gum*! *Gum*!" the gong made an indescribable sound. It shouted as the town crier Ekwechi beats it with an iron rod.

The gong played, the vibrations immediately quieted the minds of the villagers as they were passing by. They gazed in awe and silence as he spoke.

"Oh yes! Listen the good people of Amagwu village," he played the gong again. "*Gum*! *Gum*! *Gum*! Listen *o*," Ekwechi shouted again, "The good people of Amagwu, The Igwe said he expects everybody both young and old alike at the palace tomorrow morning for calamity is about to befall on the land," he said and continued to play the sound as he took to the east direction, spreading the news.

The villagers started making noise immediately **they** heard him say calamity. The sounds of their discussion echoed in the air as they took different routes to **their homes**.

Before the cock crowed for the fourth time, everybody in Amagwu woke up from their sleeps, and hastily ate their food. Though, the news of the two white men and a black had gone viral in Amagwu, the villagers wanted to go and see the 'white ghost' as they were referred to. The existence of Nicolas and Bryan confused the villagers for they were naive. At eight in the morning, they gathered at the Igwe's palace waiting for the king's arrival. No sooner than later, the Igwe arrived with his two wives and guards standing at their sides with glowing machetes. They stood up to greet their king chanting Igwe!

Igwe! Igwe! The king waved continuously in appreciation. The king got to his seat, tucked his long gown and sat down.

After waiting several minutes, he nodded with his head.

"My good people of Amagwu!" the Igwe called.

"Igwe*ee*!" the crowd echoed.

The king appreciated them for honoring his call.

"*Ku, ku, ku*!" he cleared his throat. I called you so we can deal with the calamity that has befallen on this community."

The people started murmuring, but the king's guard signaled them to uphold tranquility while the king was speaking. They gave the king a listening ear. He said, "From the history of this village, from hitherto, our village has never witnessed foreign spirits in this land. Is this not a trying message to a send (Check the grammar please) to us that we need to appeal to the gods for protection?" The Igwe said with an expression of worry on his face. "We may have heard how the White Spirits were wandering in Amagwu last Eke day. Thank the gods we saw them before they could've unleashed their wicked plans on our people."

He signaled the guards to get Nicolas and Bryan before the villagers. Two of the guards went and brought them, dragging them to the place the villagers gathered.

"Abomination!" the villagers shouted surprisingly when they saw them.

Villagers who couldn't see the men kept stretching their necks to view. They stood with their hands tied behind their backs. The men gave the villagers a long gaze. The king cleared his throat in.

"My people, we'll give these spirits a chance to tell us who they are? Where they come from? And, why they are here?"

He ordered the guards to untie them, and motioned for them to come closer to the people.

"Please, tell us everything, especially and why you're in my land," he said again.

Nicolas' fixed his eyes above the peoples head, thanked the king for giving them the opportunity to explain who they were and what brought them to Amagwu-Nze. He began to speak to them though he spoke through Walter Eric who was an Igbo man. Many people laughed at his dialect and the way he used words strangely.

"My name is Nicolas Lupe and my colleague is Bryan Wiggins. Walter Eric here is your Ibo brother. We're from the United State of America."

"Ewo! Spirits from America," the people shouted.

Nicolas continued, "I'm a medical doctor by profession, a fertility specialist and my colleague is a graduate student of reproductive endocrinology."

The villagers had a confused look of expression on their faces. They would shout whenever they heard a new word. The Onowu stood up, greeted the king and said, to the villagers, "Sorry, white spirits," he called, please all these words you mentioned were confusing because we've never heard them or make use of them in our entire lives. The only one I remember you say was fertility. Please, tell Igwe and the people what fertility is?" He sat back.

Nicolas smiled when Eric interpreted what he said, "Oh! You mean fertility?" He inquired, "I'm sorry you are not familiar with those words but let me explain them for a better understanding," he pleaded. "Fertility is just the natural capability to produce children. Least I forget, we're meant to be in Ghana by now, but we lost our way when we were traveling, fortunately, here we are. We're on a mission of helping the married couples in Ghana regain their fertility. We learned the country is facing many infertility issues," he said.

The Onowu became annoyed, he stood angrily.

"Why are you confusing us the white spirits? You said it's fertility why infertility? Please, our king wants to get a grasp of what you meant by infertility."

Nicolas apologized again and continued, "Infertility means if one cannot become pregnant at certain parameters. Since we've seen ourselves here, we consider it necessary to help curb infertility in this village. First, I must let you know the causes of infertility, so you take precautions," Nicolas boldly said.

They sat as they gazed in awed silence confused.

"The causes of infertility are; pelvic inflammatory diseases, endometriosis or fibroids, ovulation disorders, too much alcohol, and unhealthy body weight.

"Shut up!" The Igwe said angrily. "My people," he called.

"Igwe...!" they echoed.

"We know from the history of this village that it's the gods who give us children. They give those that deserve it and will not give you a child when either you or some wicked act is attached to your generation," the king boldly said.

"Yes Igwe!" they replied.

"These White Spirits are telling us now the gods are wrong," he said with an expression of sadness in his face.

"*Aru!*" the elders shouted as they knock the gnarled staffs on the ground.

"What exactly are you going to do if you claim to be wiser than the gods?" The king asked furiously.

Nicolas nodded with his head, thanked the Igwe again and continued.

"We're in Africa because we've medicines that would treat infertility so that the woman can conceive.

Hearing this, Ejikeme became excited, and prayed for the gods of the Igwe to accept their proposal to help the community.

This time, the Igwe rouse angrily.

"Incredible!" He shouted. "Are you a god?" he inquired.

Nicolas nodded in disagreement.

"We're physicians that help solve human problems through the vast knowledge we receive from learning," Bryan answered with the interpretation from Eric.

"From the history, it is the gods that gives children. Do you know the implication of what you just said?" The king asked, "Thank the gods that we've stopped spilling blood, or I would have had your meat given to the dogs," the king said angrily.

The villagers continued murmuring when the king was speaking. Ejikeme accepted all that Nicolas and Bryan said. He kept quiet because he had no right to question the king's judgment. They say the king's judgment is final.

"My people, my ear is not bigger, we heard what brought these spirits here. They're on a quest meant for the gods alone. As the king of this community, I declare that I do not want to see them in Amagwu kingdom again."

"Yes o…!" the people echoed in unison in support of the king.

The king ordered the guards to take them to the road that has seven routes, so that they can take any direction they wish and disappear from their village. The guard dragged them to the road, and left them there. They became confused of which path to take. Being atheists, they believed the law of nature will see them through.

Chapter Five

Nicolas Lupe and Bryan Wiggins became confused standing on the seven roads. They didn't know which path to follow. Eric was like a sheep that was to use for a sacrifice. He only awaits orders from his masters. Their guts were strong. They still believed that each route they should take will have villagers that will give them a warm welcome, unlike the insults and humiliations they received from the people of Amagwu, who they believe their actions is due to their naivety and reluctance to accept change. They decided to take any route instead of standing there doing nothing. Fortunately, they took a route that led to the Akpuato village. The question becomes if Akpuato will welcome them or naively chase them away like the Amagwu people. They kept walking on the narrow bosky road. Having walked half the road, they met with Okpalaugo. The drunkard staggers as he approached. When Okpalaugo got to them, he became excited. His grandfather had told him stories about the white men when he was alive. It was as if the alcohol pumping in him cleared in his eyes. He lay on the ground as he continued shouting, "*Ndi ocha! Ndi ocha!*"

Nicolas and Bryan became confused, but they were happy that at least he did not run when he saw them. This meant to them that the Akpuato were civilized. Bryan held his hand, and helped him stand up.

"*Nwa onye ocha* touched me!" he said with happiness in his face.

He requested to take them to his house. They demanded to see the king first, learning from what they experienced in Amagwu. People will always say that experience is the best teacher. Okpalaugo agreed to take them to the king's palace. They got to the palace hut painted with olden symbolography and carvings on its walls. The palace guards positioned themselves in a manner as to take good guard of the palace. It is a popular misnomer for the people of Igbo-etiti to refer to the whites as White Spirits. They got to the palace door mouth; the palace guard stopped them, and inquired to know why they came. Okpalaugo angrily replied to the guard to go and tell the king that he has visitors. They were still exchanging words tumultuously when the king heard their voice from the hut. He sent another guard that stood beside him to go and inquire what the problem was. He got back to the king with a message that two White Spirits and an Ibo claiming to be white including Okpalaugo the drunkard have come to see him. The Igwe instructed him to allow them in.

"Igwe may you live long!" Okpalaugo said.

"Good day Igwe!" the men echoed.

Bravo to these white men, few days of being in Igbo-etiti community, and they learnt how to say Igwe.

Igwe with his mouth opened to his jaw, responded, "Welcome."

"Young men who are you and how can we help you?" the Igwe inquired.

Nicolas took a bow, and thanked the Igwe. Speaking through Eric he explained vividly to the Igwe who they were and what brought them to his community. This time, Nicolas acted more wisely because he never told the king that they've been to Amagwu. The Igwe without hesitation accepted their proposal but told them he'll have their heads given to the dogs if he discovered they have hidden motives. Nicolas and Bryan promised the king they'll not do anything that will harm the kingdom.

The king thanked Okpalaugo for bringing the visitors to him. He told one of the maidens to take Okpalaugo to the quarters, give him anything he wants to eat or drink. He called the guard and ordered him to prepare a room for their visitors and make them comfortable. Nicolas and Bryan with perpetual stupefaction thanked the king, and they followed the guards to their room. The Igwe told one of the guards to tell the town crier to sound the gong. Tell everybody in Akpuato that they're needed at the king's palace by six in the morning the next day. The town crier followed the king's order and sent the message to the people at about five in the evening that day. The villagers ran in, thinking of why the king requested for their presence urgently.

* * *

The day after the town crier had spread the message of Igwe's call to the people of Akpuato. At six-thirty in the evening, Nneka hurriedly went to Nwanyimma's hut. When she got to the hut, Nwanyimma was in front of the old kitchen preparing her dinner. Her stepmother did not allow her to eat with them. She wore a gown that was below her knees and sat on a small wooden chair, pounding the melon seeds in a mortal as she raised her hand up and down. The sound of the pestle contacting the mortal echoed in the air *Gbom! Gbom! Gbom!* Nneka excited got to where she sat pounding, greeted and offered her help to cut the vegetable on the plate. She also helped her prepare the food while they talked.

"*Eem*, Mma, I know it's barely two months plus and you'll leave me in this village," said Nneka.

"My dear thank the gods, I'm so happy because I can't wait to go back to my husband. Oh! Ejikeme my husband, I wonder how that innocent man have been cooking all this while," Nwanyimma said.

"My dear, I'm so happy for you," she said smiling, "*Ehe*! Least I forget, something spectacular brought me to your house this evening," Nneka said with expression of happiness.

"Whatever it is, I think it is important," Nwanyimma said.

"You heard the town carrier some hour ago, or didn't you?" Nneka inquired.

"I did," Nwanyimma said. "What about it?" she asked,

"My dear, I have selected best of my cloth for the gathering tomorrow." I must make sure I'll appear on my best outfit so every suitor present will succumb," Nneka said smiling.

"Ah! Nneka, you won't kill the person you'll still help and bury," said Nwanyimma. "We're only hear from the king about the new Yam Festival or any special occasion of the village," she smiled and said. "Suitors come when it's time for them to sister," she added.

"How long?" she said as she stood from the wooden chair, "Nne *lekene m anya*, I'm not getting any younger, *nwanyi na agbadazi agbada*," Nneka angrily said as she turned half round swaying her waist.

"Nnem don't worry too much; remember too much a worry is like adding salt to the injury ," said Nwanyimma.

"I heard you my sister; at least, I've to look good tomorrow. It's one reason I come, cook fast and help me arrange this hair," she said pointing at her new plaits with a black thread.

"Oh I never knew you made hair, it's good dear, who plaited it?" Nwanyimma asked.

"*Eem*! It's Ojiugo, we know she's the best at plaiting hair," said Nneka.

"It's true my dear. The gods blessed her with good handy work," said Nwanyimma.

They finished the cooking, ate and were satisfied.

Nneka stood up to go because it was already getting late. Nwanyimma saw her off and came back.

At six in the morning, everybody arrived at Igwe's palace to know why he requested for their presence. Soon enough, the Igwe came from the north side of the hut with his family, maidens and bodyguards armed heavily. The people seeing him stood up echoing, "Igwe! Igwe! Igwe!"

The Igwe appreciated them for honoring his call, told them why he had sent for them. The people of Akpuato became happy for the latest development except Uyachi, the chief priest who was furious as rage boiled through his body. He paced round, knocked his staff of authority on the ground. This staff member had different colors of cloth. He came to the king, nodded, waited, looked at the crowd, turned again and said,

"My king, don't you think it's a slap at the gods for going to another god for help?" Uyachi said worriedly.

"Mouth piece of the gods, patience, it was the gods that brought these young men for us," said the king.

The chief priest nodded in dismay, left the gathering in vexation. One of the guards sent by Nicolas whispered to the Igwe that the White Spirits were ready to see the women.

Nicolas Lupe, Bryan Wiggins and Walter Eric were in one room in the Igwe's palace. They used it for the medical purposes that brought them to Africa. The Igwe announced to couples married for a long time who have difficulties in conceiving, and maidens from fifteen years, to see the men. He told the guards to see that tranquility is upheld why doing so. He thanked them and left the gathering. People that were not concerned took their different routes and went home to begin their day's work. For Nwanyimma, she was happy; she believed the gods sent them. Nneka who was so eager to see the White Spirit jumped off her seat and filed on the line. She was the eleventh person on the queue. Nwanyimma stood behind her. The men began to see the women, and them. They counsel each after the test, gave and prescribed drugs. Nneka got in, Nicolas' body changed. He became mentally distracted but managed to take hold of himself, he motioned to her to see Bryan for her test and drugs. His system would not allow him to do otherwise. He kept gazing at her. She never knew what was happening with Nicolas. She got her drugs and left. Nwanyimma the next in the queue went in. Nicolas tested her, told her that she had an infection which has been preventing the egg from reaching the fallopian tube.

Hearing this, she became worried, asked if there is any solution to her case.

"Oh yes!" said Nicolas.

She took a brief breathe of relief and said,

"Thank the gods."

Nicolas gave her some drugs, calmed her by telling her that she'll get pregnant soon. She became so excited as she rose, knelt down and the thanked Nicolas. Nicolas helped her stand up. She left; more women in the queue got their medications. When they finished for the day, they told the king they want to tour around the village the next day. Without hesitation, the king granted their request. He ordered one of the bodyguards to take them around the village. Nicolas and Bryan were in their room talking when Nicolas told Bryan the experience he had seeing one of the maidens. They sat on the reclining chairs in the room. Nicolas sat leaning backward on the chair. Bryan sat close to the edge of the chair, had his jotter on his hand writing. It was his usual manner of writing saying that he'll publish a story about their journey to Africa. Eric lay on the bamboo bed with pricked ear listening to their discussion.

"Bryan," said Nicolas.

"Yes sir!" answered Bryan as he turned to look at Nicolas.

"I've seen a young woman I love in this community; I haven't experienced this for a longtime. There was a slow motion in my body," Nicolas said worriedly.

Bryan smiling said,

"The village got damsels, blacks are beautiful sir. The problem is, we'll be leaving soon. Meanwhile, I do not think any African woman would marry a total stranger like us."

"Yea!" said Nicolas, I think I have to do something about it, I love the woman, and when I say it, I mean it."

Bryan still smiling said,

"Wow! Sir, I must confess that you like this woman. Why don't you talk to her to know if she feels the same way you do.

Nicolas smiled, "That was why I asked the king to let us tour the village tomorrow. We'll call Okalago (as he pronounced

Okpalaugo) so he helps us fetch her."

"Master is in love with an African," Bryan said smiling. "If I may ask what's the name of this lucky woman master?" He asked.

"You know the woman I motioned to see you for test?" Nicolas reminded him.

"Yes, I do", answered Bryan.

"Check the place you wrote their names, Nicolas said pointing as Bryan opened his jotter to check for Nneka's name.

Oh! Neka," (he pronounced). He wrote Nneka's name wrongly, she saw the name wrongly spelt but she's not able to correct it because there was nothing like formal education in that period. They teach them through myths and stories from the old people. They gather them and tell them stories before they go to bed.

"What a coincidence!" Nicolas snapped as he went closer to see the name. "Nature indeed brought us here," he smiled.

"Master, it's indeed a coincidence, but I hope she's not married because I learnt Africans engage in early marriage," Bryan said.

"My instinct is telling me she is not," Nicolas said.

At about seven-thirty in the evening, a bodyguard brought food for them, served them and stayed back until they finished eating and then he took the plates back. They had little discussion and went to bed.

In the morning, Nicolas and Bryan got ready for the tour, **and informed** the king. One of the bodyguards escorted them. **They wouldn't have gone out with Eric if not for interpretation of the strange language as they took it to be.** On the door mouth, they saw Okpalaugo coming. They were happy **seeing** him, because they wanted to tell the guard to take them to his hut first. When Okpalaugo got close he greeted them,

"*Nwa onye ocha ana m ekele!*" **he** greeted as he bowed down in respect.

They exchange greetings, and took him along for the tour. Nicolas told Okpalaugo how he felt about Nneka. Okpalaugo was happy and told them that he'll help him and make Nneka agree to his proposal. They toured around the village as Bryan

was busy taking pictures.

Two days later, Nicolas already told Nneka how he felt about her, Nneka accepted his proposal. Her fear was how she's going to marry a total stranger she knew nothing about. Secondly, she thought how she'll leave Akpuato for another country that she has never been to before. "It's better-off a man from another village but in this Igbo-etiti", she said. The whole issue confused her. At first, she said she needed to confide with Nwanyimma before she tells her mother.

"*Hum*! My mother saw them as a foreign spirit. She wanted me to marry but not a total stranger this time."

She stood up, wore her cloth, locked the door and left to see Nwanyimma.

She got to Nwanyimma's hut, and explained everything to her.

"*Hum*! Is confusing," Nwanyimma said, "*nne m*, do you love him?" Nwanyimma asked softly.

"Yes I do! But I'm still confused," Nneka said.

"Why confused?" she asked Nneka.

"My dear is still like a fairy tale, first, falling in love with a total stranger. Secondly getting married to him and leaving the country, a country far from Akpuato," she said with expression of worry on her face.

"My sister, I understand you," Nwanyimma said. "But you must understand that when we love, we learn to sacrifice," she said.

"Oh! What would I have done without a friend like you?" Nneka asked. "You are full of experiences," she added. "Another problem posed here is my mother," she included.

"Your mother what about her?" Nwanyimma inquired.

"Do you think she'll allow the wedding to hold?" Nneka asked.

"You are to decide," Nwanyimma advised, "Your mother isn't the one marrying," she added. "Give her reasons you're marrying him, when she sees your good reasons she'll accept," Nwanyimma said.

"What can I do without you Mma?" she said embracing her, stood up and took her leave while Mma saw her off.

• * *

Few days later, about five children from Ekpof village went to Okofia or big bush in the neighbouring village to fetch firewood. They carried with them machetes and hoes because they also have in mind of hunting before getting firewood. When they got to the big bush, they decided to fetch firewood first before the hunting. They spread through the bush in search of firewood. A boy of about twelve years saw something that looked like a house covered with dust and leaves that fall off the trees. He alerted the other children who came and struck by amazement. For them, the gods decided to provide a house for them in the bush. This was the car abandoned by Nicolas and his cohort. They ran to the village and informed the elders. After many days of rituals by the village chief priest, the car was made a tourists area. It was well decorated and was named, *"obi chi,* or house of the gods,"* People from other villages also came for sightseeing in Ekpof village.

* * *

It remains three weeks for Mma to go back to Amagwu village. On Eke Day, her husband decided to secretly pay her a visit, he planned to spend the night with Mma, his wife. At four in the evening, he left for his journey to Akpuato. He brought many gifts with him. When he arrived, Mma became excited, embraced him and gave him a warm welcome. She hurriedly ran around to prepare food for him.

"I must prepare the best meal for him because he deserves it," she said happily.

She finished cooking at seven-fifteen in the evening and served the food on tray pan. They both ate to their satisfaction. At nine in the evening, they went to bed. They turned off the light and made love the first time after three years. There was a heavy downpour that night that made them enjoy the night even more like never before.

In the morning, Ejikeme prepared and went back to Amagwu village. Nobody in Amagwu village knew that he had gone to Akpuato to visit his wife. If they've known, Ejike would have to dance the dance of the spirit. One week after Ejike's visit to

Nwanyimma, she started noticing some changes in her body.

She became afraid because such had never happened to her before. One afternoon, she was sleeping when Nneka paid her a visit as usual. It surprised her seeing Mma sleeping by that time of the day. What she had never seen her do since they became friends. She tapped her on the leg as she called her name to wake her up. When she woke up, her face was covered

with sweat. She raised her long blouse to clean the sweat.

"Mma, hope you're well?" Nneka asked as she sat beside her. "*Mtchew,*" Mma hissed, "I do not understand my body these days. I do not want to take any herbs now because I'm not ready for those concoctions," Nwanyimma said.

"Oh *Nwanyi oma,*" Nneka shouted, "Even your face is swollen. Maybe we need to see Nico and Bran." (She shortly pronounced). "They might know what to do."

She nodded in Affirmation, and stood up;

"Let me quickly wash my face so we'll get going before it gets out of control."

She went to the iron pail, and washed her face with the water in it. When she finished, they left to the Igwe's palace to see the physicians.

They got there, following the symptoms she mentioned; Nicolas told her that she's pregnant. She didn't believe what her ears heard because it was too heavy for her. With her month opened to her jaws, she shouted.

"What?"

Nneka became excited; she kept thanking the gods for having answered her friend's prayers. Tears of joy welled down her plump chin. They both went back happily.

* **

Two weeks later, the physicians including the Onowu went to Nneka's hut to pay her bride price. Her mother accepted them after much struggle; they paid the bride price and performed every marriage right. After paying the bride price, Nicolas went to the king to fix a date for a traditional wedding ritual since they're to leave the village as soon as possible. The United States government responded to the mail they sent to come for their aid. The time the government gave them was one week. Nneka was happy that at last she will be happily married. Her worries were leaving behind everything in Akpuato. The king fixed the date for the traditional wedding to take place. The next Eke market day, Nicolas and Nneka traditionally united. Two days after their traditional wedding, the delegates sent to pick them arrived. They left Akpuato and happily promised to plead with their government to send them teachers for formal education. The villagers including their king were happy. They told them that they'd gladly welcome formal education with open hands because their lives were practical evidence of what formal education can do.

* **

It was the third week Nwanyimma had gone back to her husband in Amagwu. This book cannot describe Ejikeme's happiness seeing his wife pregnant. He always played around with her stomach saying that he wants to have a discussion with a baby in it. Nwanyimma thought her pregnancy will make everything get back to normal. Unfortunately, it turned out the other way around.

Everybody in Amagwu already heard that Nwanyimma was pregnant, and believed that she carried the pregnancy from Akpuato to their village. Perhaps, her husband is not responsible for her pregnancy as they always said.

Mazi Ikeobi on hearing the story said he won't go with a mere gossip from people, he decided to go to Ejikeme's hut to see him. It was five in the evening. Nwanyimma was preparing night food for herself and her husband. Suddenly, Mazi Ikeobi

walked in. Seeing him she greeted.

"*Nna anyi noo*!" she said standing up.

Mazi Ikeobi took a lasting gaze at her.

"So it's true," he shouted surprisingly.

"What's the problem *nna anyi*?" Nwanyimma asked.

"Who is your *nna*?" he inquired. "So you came back to this village with another man's baby eeh? This witch, you decided to ruin my brother's life. You also succeeded in bringing shame to this family," he added.

"*Nna anyi*, I've not done anything wrong, perhaps the baby belongs to my husband," she said calmly.

"Abomination! *Aru*!" he shouted as anger crept into his voice. "When will you stop your lies?" he asked. "You forgot that for three years, (he displayed with his hands), *afo ato* (he counted) *otu, abuo, ato*. My brother wasn't with you and you came back pregnant claiming it to be his." He was still talking when Ejike came from the back porch of the hut, carrying firewood. With his mouth open to his jaw he shouted

"*Tufiakwa*!" he cursed. So you're even fetching firewood for her? Nursing pregnancy that belonged to another man, tell me Ejike, is it how foolish you've grown?" Mazi Ikeobi said angrily.

Ejike became upset on hearing this, he shouted at him and told him not to insult his wife again. Nwanyimma drew closer to her husband whose temper was flaring **and tried** to calm him down.

"Listen, flies that fail to listen will surely go down the grave with the corpse," Mazi Ikeobi said as he turned and left angrily.

Ejike held his wife close and embraced her warmly. He calmed her by telling her that he would never allow anyone to insult nor humiliate her again as long he is alive. Tears streamed down Nwanyimma's cheeks while her husband tried to put her together.

* * *

Two days later, mama Ezekwesiri excited on hearing her friend Nwanyimma was back from Akpuato decided to pay her a visit. She took with her some gifts in a **basket. She** carried with her three yams, garden eggs, pepper, cocoyam's and groundnut. She got those because they just harvested some days before

Nwanyimma came back. She balanced the basket on her head with a simple cloth shaped into a ring. When she got to the

door mouth, she shouted,

"*Kpam*! *Kpam*! *Kpam*! Who's in this house?"

Nwanyimma was deeply asleep; her husband had gone to the farm.

"*Kpam*! *Kpam*! *Kpam*!" Mama Ezekwesiri shouted again.

This time Nwanyimma came out with her brown face covered with sweat. Seeing her, Mama Ezekwesiri who was balancing a basket on her head started clapping.

"Big madam," she said with excitement on her face.

"Oh! Mama Eze, welcome," said Nwanyimma.

"This woman so you're this beautiful?" said mama Ezekwesiri as she squatted to bring down the basket. The cloth fell from her head to her back. She picked it, put it inside the basket, and drew it closer to embrace Nwanyimma.

"I missed you my friend," Mama Eze said.

"Oh! My dear, the same *o*, how's Eze?" Nwanyimma inquired.

"My dear Eze is fine, he ought to have followed me, but I don't know when he left to the playground."

"Oh! Children and playing, their simple world is better," said Nwanyimma as she went in and brought a bench under a mango tree at the front porch of her hut. Mama Eze was still standing at the front porch of the hut. Mma came back, brought an old cloth on the lower roof of the hut to clean the bench. Mama Eze told her to take those items inside.

"This is the little I can afford my dear, please take it as you saw them," Mama Eze added.

"*Ewo*!" she shouted surprisingly, "Mama Eze, all these for me? Thank you and may the gods bless you." "*Amin o!*" Mama Eze said.

Nwanyimma took the basket inside, put those items on her own basket and brought mama Eze's basket out. They sat on the bench under the mango tree.

Mma Ezekwesiri cleared her throat in wholesome nature, waited, and called her by name.

"Mma my friend, I'm happy for you. Tell me, how it happened?" She inquisitively asked.

"*Hum*!" Nwanyimma shouted, "The gods decided to put a smile on my embittered face. I now understood the sayings, who are we to question the gods in their makings?" She added.

She explained how everything happened. How the white men came to Akpuato and touched lives, including hers. Mama Ezekwesiri told her the white men came to Amagwu. They rejected, humiliated and dragged them out of this village. "The gods are wise!" she said. "So they later brought them to your destination?" She surprisingly asked.

"Yes *o*! My dear the gods showed me how they work. I didn't hear they were here. Amagwu will always remain blind for refusing to welcome development," Nwanyimma said in a calm and unhurried voice. "I pray for the future of our children," she included. "Do you know the two men pleaded with their government to bring teachers to Akpuato who'll help them

with formal education?"

"Formal education? Gods of our land, what did we do to have chased the good coming to our land?' She asked worriedly. "I've heard stories from my father of formal education. It isn't in

Africa. It's available to those in developed sides of the continent. I heard from him that formal education is costly, expensive to get." Mama Eze included.

"Really?" Nwanyimma asked.

Mama Eze nodded in affirmation.

"So they decided to give people of Akpuato formal education pricelessly?" Mama Eze asked.

"Yes my dear!" **she** replied, "If my child becomes of schoolage as they told us. She'll go from here to get the education that made the government of Nico and Bran listened to them," Mma said.

"Nico and Bran, who are they?" Mama Eze inquired.

"They're the white men the people of Amagwu naively sent out of their village."

"*Hum*! My dear, the education shaped them. They amazed me the day Igwe brought them to speak to us. A day before they sent them out of the village. The words they pronounced,

I never heard in my entire life."

"*Eem*! *Eem*!" she ran in thought as she tried to remember the words. "Yes!" She shouted as she recalled *facality* and *infacality* (she wrongly pronounced).

Nwanyimma burst out with laughter,

"Ha, ha, ha! Mama Eze, it's fertility and infertility not facality."

Mama Eze became surprise Nwanyimma pronounced those words correctly. She inquired to know how she learnt it knowing too well that she had not attended any formal institution of learning, nevertheless, none in Igbo-etiti at the time. Nwanyimma told her Nicolas and Bryan spent time teaching them. Mama Eze pointed blame on their king and archaic village custom. They engaged in a lengthy discussion that day. At about five in the evening, mama Eze went home. Nwanyimma prepared food for her husband. She sat on a wooden chair inside the kitchen and began to cut the vegetables. She paused, held her stomach as she talked to her unborn child, "I promise to give you formal education, so you'll be like Nicolas and Bryan."

Chapter Six

The news that Nwanyimma was pregnant had gone wide. The people of Amagwu had heard it was

Akpuato people that later accepted Nicolas and Bryan. This made them to keep saying that White Spirits impregnated Nwanyimma. They didn't believe she would ever be pregnant at her age. They pointed fingers at her and called her all sorts of annoying and irritating names.

Two days later, the elders invited Ejikeme to come and explain why he bluntly refused to send Nwanyimma away knowing she was pregnant from the foreign spirits. Five elders sat at the village square at eight in the morning. The sun was still rising from the East; they sat waiting for Ejikeme to arrive.

The elders were Mazi Ikeobi, Ikeokwu, Okonkwo, Nweke and the big *achi* tree formed canopies that shaded one from the direct sun. They sat on the wooden planks set in form of a bench on the large roots of the **achi** tree and they talked. Soon, they saw Ejike coming from a distance, **wearing black** trouser and plain chieftaincy attire. He held a traditional hat on his left hand.

"Oh! Here he comes," said Ikeokwu as he pointed at the direction to which Ejikeme was coming from.

He got to the elders, greeted them, and apologized for coming late.

"Please my elders forgive me for keeping you waiting," he said as he bent to sit on a space left for him.

The elders accepted his apologies; Mazi Ikeobi cleared his throat in a wholesome nature.

"*Ku, ku, ku*" waited, and thanked the elders for honoring the call, and introduced the subject of the gathering. "*Eem*! Ejike," he called as he cleared his throat again "*Ku, ku, ku*." We the elders of this village will not seat and watch something go wrong. Our people said "the elder don't sit and watch while the child is going astray. If he didn't do anything, the elder is punishable by the gods."

"*O bu eziokwu*!" echoed the elders.

"We called you here because you are a brother and a son to us. Tell us why you decide to take the bull by the horn," Mazi Ikeobi asked.

"*Gbam*!" the elders shouted knocking their staff on the ground in affirmation.

"This is confusing," Ejike said as he tried to sit well.

"My elders let the air show the fowl's buttock and stop prolonging the issues. Making it hard for ordinary man like me to understand," Ejike said.

"*Ah*!" Ikeokwu shouted as he rose quickly in anger, "what don't you understand? *Eeh*!" he said.

"Everything, *kpo okwu aha*," he said.

Ikeokwu took his seat as Okonkwo stood up. He cleared his throat and nodded with his head and said "Ejike my son, we invited you here because we've your interest at heart. We thought it was high time you left Mma, You and I know the pregnancy belonged to the White Spirits. Haven't you thought about this?" He inquired as he sat down.

Ejike became angry, embittered, his temper flared as he quickly stood and took a lasting gaze at the elders.

"It's obvious poor retched elders like you who do not have any useful engagements this early morning, but just sit and gallivant on issues you don't know."

The elders with their mouth opened to their jaws echoed uniformly,

"What?"

Nweke rose quickly as anger crept in his voice. He told him to excogitate on what the elders told him, he'll see their importance. "If you give deaf ears to them, you'll suffer the imminent alone. Nevertheless, our people said that the grasshopper that runs in the mist of fowls ends up in the land of spirits," he said and sat down when he finished saying this.

"You sycophants, what do you want me to give a thought to?"

Mazi Ikeobi rose angrily, "I cannot sit and watch you insult me and the elders. Have you lost your mind?" Mazi Ikeobi asked pointing his staff at him. "I thought you are wise. Have you lost your acumen? Father was proud of you when he was alive, but it hurts to see you fail him," Mazi Ikeobi said.

"Thanks but no thanks," Ejike said. "I must say this, do not invite me for this discussion with no basis for judgment." He was about to complete his statement when Okonkwo caught in anger said; "Or what? No tell me, what will happen? Have us thrown to the dungeon? Give our heads to the dogs?"

Ejikeme left them without a word as he boiled in anger. The animals that came across his path sensed his bitterness. The elders left angrily to their different destinations ranting on how to deal with him.

* * *

Three months later, the United States Government sent two learned and erudite personnel to Akpuato. They sent them to help them acquire formal education as requested by Nicolas Lupe and Bryan Wiggins. The government supplied them with learning materials that'll help the villagers learn fast and gave them six years to stay in Akpuato and train teachers that will take their position before they live. The people of Akpuato became happy for the development brought to them by the two young men. They became the first to enjoy formal education in Africa.

Ghana ought to be the ones to boast of this development but their *chi, or personal god* did not affirm. The Igwe accommodated them in the palace. The two teachers sent to Akpuato are Nicole Cooley and Larry Randy. Nicole Cooley is a tall middle-aged woman probably in her early forties and taught the 11th grade in Silver Creek High School, Longmont. She won the best teacher in Colorado teacher's day award and was known for her friendliness and geniality for her students. She's married to Adams Cooley, a leading research lecturer in the Department of Biotechnology in Colorado State University.

Larry Randy is also a lecturer in Colorado State University. He was nominated by the University for his love of community service. He's a man in his late forties who is married with kids. They were happy being in Africa but they feared that Africa had no basis for formal education that they had to start from the scratch with training. Secondly, when they came to Akpuato, they toured around the village and they found out they worshiped different gods. They were devoted Christians. First, they promised to accept their religion as a way of making them peak interest. They planned to talk to them about the wrongs of their traditional religion when they get formal experience. The people of Akpuato happily accepted them with open hands. They were eager to learn so that they'll be like them. The elders would say if they won't learn the so-called foreign education, our children must since it's priceless.

How news spread. It's all over Amagwu, the news of the arrival of the two White Spirits as they refer to them. Everyone of Igbo-etiti heard of the arrival of these two White Spirits for formal education. People became excited when they heard the news. At least, development started with their people as they say. Amagwu is the only community that envies the people of Akpuato. They regard them as being naïve and weak to allow total strangers to bring a new culture in the form of what they call formal education.

One month later, mama Ezekwesiri came to see her friend Mma as usual. Nwanyimma was happy upon seeing her. She's the only one who cared to take care of her since she was pregnant. She brought old gowns she wore during her pregnancy time. When she arrived, Nwanyimma was plucking peppers from her small garden. She got to the front porch of the hut; she did not see Nwanyimma, "*Onye no n'ulo a?*" she asked.

Nwanyimma was busy collecting the peppers. She walked to her at the back of the hut, and saw her plucking the peppers.

"Oh!Mama Eze you came?"Nwanyimma asked as she plucked the last pepper.

"*Nne asi m ka m bia mara ka I mere,*" she said in Igbo language. "*Oh*! It's kind of you my dear," Nwanyimma said smiling.

"What would I have done without you?" she said.

"It's nothing my dear!" Mama Eze said, "You need somebody by your side. I'm here for you," she said as they went to the front porch of the hut.

They walked to the mango tree and sat on the bench talking. Mama Eze brought the three gowns and presented them to Nwanyimma. She was happy seeing those gowns because she planned on giving Mama Eze money on Afo day to select gowns for her at the market.

"You don't know you've cut some expenses for me," she said expressing joy on her face. Mama Eze told her that since she's not bearing again; it would be of no use to keep those gowns in her house.

"*Ehe*!" Mama Eze shouted as she tapped her at the laps, "Have you heard of the latest development in your village?" she inquisitively asked.

"*Oh*! It's no longer new, I heard about it and I'm proud of Akpuato," Nwanyimma said as she smiled.

"*Nne m*, I'd like Ezekwesiri to start as soon as possible. The problem is the ban by Igwe," Mama Eze said with a look of worry.

"Amagwu should swallow their pride and grab a lifetime opportunity?" Nwanyimma said.

"Exactly!" shouted mama Eze as she stood up from where she sat. "They've been bragging, and claiming that they're the oldest village in this Igbo-etiti. Amagwu will not learn anything good from Akpuato they say. I think it's time we start looking for the black goat before night falls," she said as she unties and reties her wrapper knotting it twice around her waist, and then sat down.

"Mama Eze, you see this unborn child, once she's of age she must go and learn formal education because we do not know what the future holds for our children," Nwanyimma said. "Who knows if their generation will be known formal education? Our people say that big things start small," Nwanyimma added.

"Nnem, we're praying for the gods to open the eyes of our Igwe and the elders, so they'll know it's our children's future that is at stake here. We cannot sacrifice their future, their happiness for superiority's sake," Mama Eze said.

"My dear, hope with time he'll discover the harm he's doing to himself and his subjects," Mma said.

After much discussion, mama Ezekwesiri went home while Nwanyimma saw her off. She came back; took the pepper, poured them on a tray pan and kept it on the lower roof of the hut.

People of Akpuato embraced the foreign formal education with enthusiasm. Okpalaugo is the first to come to sit on the front chair. Mrs. Cooley and Mr. Randy gave them a scheme for the session's work.

Thank the gods' women of Akpuato showed interest to the formal education. Their men preferred the bar where they usually go for sweet palm wine to the so-called foreign education. They were happy with the development but preferred that their wives and children would go and learn. They believed palm wine had taken the place of formal education in their cerebrium. According to the scheme that day, they have the right pronunciation. They taught them how to pronounce words. It wasn't easy for Akpuato people that day. Most, especially the older ones found it difficult to re-twist their tongues to produce the right pronunciation. Wow! Mrs. Cooley and Mr. Randy are teachers I'm proud of. They devised a means for easy pronunciation. After lessons that day, Akpuato people were happy. They can boast of pronouncing the English words well. They took their different routes after the class. They kept pronouncing the words they learnt the day.

Two weeks later, it was the big market day for the Akpuato village. People from far and near come to afo Akpuato that day to buy and sell. Many people from Amagwu came to sell their farm produce. Some came to see if good was happening in Akpuato or if it's just a fairy tale. They chimed at the culture and would say will good ever come from Akpuato. At the Afo market, everybody was busy buying or selling. There were so many people in Afo Akpuato that day that if you throw a grain of sand it will not find its way to the earth again. Amagwu people walked to every nook and cranny of the market to clear their doubts. They became flabbergasted by the way Akpuato people communicated with them when they exchanged words with them. What baffled them the most was the old women speaking phonetics. They were ashamed of their dying in ignorance. About forty percent of people from Amagwu came to Afo that day. They vowed to end the hostility among them and the Akpuato people before it gets out of control. When they got to Amagwu, the elders held a clandestine meeting without telling the king. They talked how to go and make the king allow their people to learn from the White Spirits in Akpuato. They knew the king is implacable to matters like this. They decided to select elders that are well-spoken and bold enough to face the king. The elders selected to go were Nweke, Mazi Ikeobi, Ikeokwu and Okonkwo. They told them to make the Igwe see reasons to allow them to do the right before it becomes late. In the evening of that day, the elders went to the Igwe's palace to see him. When they got to the palace, the Igwe sat in his *obi* with his second wife, eating garden egg and pumpkin. When the Lolo saw the elders, she stood, greeted them. The elders greeted the Igwe echoing,

"Igwe! Igwe!" May you live long,"

The Igwe welcomed them and gave them a seat. The Lolo took the calabash and went out. The Igwe told her to get kolanut for the elders. When she brought the kolanut, they thanked the gods for life, children and peace in their community, and prayed for more blessings to come. They blessed, broke the kola nut and ate it. The Igwe inquired to know why they come to see him unannounced. Nweke stood, nodded his head as a gesture of respect , and cleared his throat in wholesome nature. He looked at the Igwe and said "Everyone likes soup with fish in it Igwe, we witnessed how the people of Akpuato have developed within some weeks of this so-called formal education. We're even afraid our children's future will suffer it if we continue being in ill with them. Igwe! I've always known you to be coherent and understandable. I know you'll understand the importance of this. I know you'll have the interest of this kingdom at heart. We the elders of this kingdom came to plead with you to allow us and our children to go to Akpuato and receive a formal education so that the people of Akpuato will not one day deny them their right, after getting this wealth of knowledge."

"*Ndi ichie ibem obu na o bughi eziokwu?*" he asked the elders.

"*Eziokwu ka ikwuru,* the elders echoed.

He thanked the king and sat down.

"Thank you, my people," the Igwe said, "I heard you and your views for the recent happenings in Akpuato village. If I may ask, have you forgotten that our people once said one shouldn't use the morning to predict a bad market? People of Akpuato accepting the so-called formal education doesn't mean they are better than us. Remember, we remain the giant stride and no son or daughter of Amagwu should be afraid of the future.

The future holds good for us," the king assured them.

The king's understanding of the matter made the elders sad. They swore to finalize everything with the king for their children to start as soon as possible. Okonkwo stood, and thanked the Igwe. He said,

"Igwe, it's better one look for a black goat in the afternoon, we're talking our children future here and the unborn. We know we shouldn't be the one reminding you of this, but we have to do it because nobody is an Island. Please Igwe do this for us," he said with worry in his face as he took his seat.

The Igwe ran in thought as everybody was calm waiting for him to take his final decision. They prayed the god's touched his heart to see some good reasons behind their visit. Soon enough, Igwe broke the silence, cleared his throat, "*Ahem*! My people, I gave a deep thought on the subject matter." The Igwe waited, casted a look at the elders and continued, "Since I started reigning in this kingdom, this is one thing you asked me to do for you. The people of Amagwu have undoubtedly been loyal to my reign. I think I'll not deny you this one request. Therefore, I king Ogueji the 6th acquiesced to your demands."

The elders applauded in happiness and thanked the king, expressing their happiness. They left the palace so excited. The news to go to Akpuato to receive formal education elated Amagwu people on hearing it. They never knew the formal education was a hard one. They thought it was going to the farm, being in enmity with the Akpuato people. Families started arranging on how their children will start the journey of another page in life. They held a meeting at the village square and agreed they'll be going in groups since Akpuato was a bit far from Amagwu. They advised the children to hide their identity from Akpuato people. They'll have them insulted if they find out that they later succumbed to their so-called western education.

Two days later, at the fourth cock crow, the children gathered at the village square. They were happy because it was their first day going to Akpuato to get formal education. They advised the older ones to take good care of the young ones. Make sure that they are complete while coming back after the day's class. They left Amagwu at six in the morning on Nkwo day. The younger children were backed by their siblings; the children without older siblings were backed by the older ones without younger siblings. There were no writing materials because they didn't have any.

At about seven-fifteen in the morning, they got to Akpuato. Children from neighboring villages had gotten to Akpuato before their arrival. Normal time for their classes is eightthirty in the morning to accommodate for people coming from far places. The class started at eight, thirty-two. The children arrived and settled. When Nicole came up to take the lesson, she greeted the children and they replied. Brandy was going around directing them while Nicole taught the lesson. It isn't easy for the Amagwu children that day. Everything is a different setting. They preferred their normal farming work to the formal education. They prayed for the day to fast-forward. Everything Nicole taught entered from the right ear and went through and out the left ear.

When Brandy was going around inspecting the children, he noticed that a good number of the students were absent minded. They're not writing and most of them came from Amagwu. He tried all he could to teach them how to write but all his effort became ineffectual. After the day's class, Brandy and Nicole stayed back to attend to some children that came for private counseling. On their way home, they talked how hard and boring formal education could be. Many of the children said they prefer farming till eternity than having them go through the hard moments of class. The older ones among them claimed the little ones by telling them that the children of Akpuato we will deride them for not coming because the system was hard for them to adapt. We need to prove to them that we're still the oldest tribe in Igbo-etiti, they said. When they got home that day, they told their parents the formal education wasn't an easy one. They encouraged them, told them they'll soon get used to it since it was just their first day.

Chapter Seven

That evening all legs were going to Ejikeme's compound immediately, as they got the news of Nwanyimma's delivery. The people going to the hut were not going because they were happy but to see if the child Nwanyimma would give birth to is Ejikeme's. Ejikeme was the happiest man in Amagwu that day. He went to Mazi Iruka the palm wine tapper and bought enough palm wine from him and the people that came to see the child.

Mazi Ikeobi and mama Ifenyinwa didn't hear the news early. Ifenyinwa announced the news to them. She happened to pass through Ejikeme's hut on her way back from the stream with her younger brother Chioye. On hearing this, they both ran on their heels to go and see what the child looked like. Mama Ifenyinwa was busy untying and retying her wrapper as she ran.

"*Nna anyi* wait for me *o!*" she shouts as they ran through the narrowing path.

They got to Ejikeme's hut and all nooks and crannies of the hut were filled with gaiety and laughter. Mazi Ikeobi called one of the women, who was talking to another and whispered, "What did she give birth to?"

The woman excitedly told him she gave birth to a baby girl.

"*O si* girl?" Mazi Ikeobi shouted.

"Yes, *nna anyi* or is anything wrong," the woman inquired.

"*Eem*! No my dear nothing is wrong, but I am happy for them," he said with a devil-may-care outlook and a stellar smile.

"Thank the gods! I'm happy for them, at least she's now like every other woman in Amagwu," the woman said happily.

"Yes, yes," said Ikeobi as he went to his wife.

She joined the women seated under the mango tree taking garden egg and dancing one after the other in joy. He got to where she stood, held her by the hand and dragged her out of the compound.

"Ogini *nna anyi*," asked Mama Ifenyinwa as she took her hand forcibly.

"Don't you have sense?" Mazi Ikeobi asked angrily.

"What's the matter trying to take what belongs to me? *Eeh*! You know after today I won't eat anything from this stingy brother of yours," she said, and stood with her two hands on her waist.

"You're a longer throat," said Mazi Ikeobi, "what's there to excite, eat and merry? I just heard she gave birth to a mere girl, *Nwata nwanyi*!" said Ikeobi as anger crept into his voice.

"*Oh*! *Gini mezie*?" Mama Ifi inquired.

"Ah! You're still asking me questions? You forgot that a female child is as been barren."

"*Ha, ha, ha*! *Ewo*! Husband, you worry a lot," she said smiling, drew closer, and held her husband by the shoulder.

"Bring your ear closer; have you forgotten that your brother is a farmer well-known in Amagwu your fatherland? You told me how your father loved him when you both were growing up because he was hardworking, look at his barn, inside there, you'll see yams of different sizes, all varieties of crops, I think we should be happy," she said as she continued smiling.

"Happy? How? Why?" he inquisitively asked.

"I know you as indolent when it comes to work," she carelessly said.

Mazi Ikeobi became annoyed when his wife said that.

"Are you insulting me or what?"

"*Mbanu di m oma,* it hasn't gotten to that, I wanted to say whether female child or no child is none of our concern. Our interest should be on that rich barn when they die. Our children won't suffer. Take a good look at our barn and you'll appreciate this."

Mazi Ikeobi's mind wandered through the empty barn of his.

"Oh! I understand you," he said smiling, "I should have trusted you with your intelligence," he added. "You mean we should not worry about whether male or female?"

"*Gbam*! That's what I'm saying."

"Come here," he said,

His wife drew closer; he gave her a warm hug.

"You're a wise woman. Please let's go home and merry because good are on their way coming."

They left while the merriment was still on. Some women volunteered to sleep in Ejike's hut that day to keep Mma and the baby company. Mama Ezekwesiri was one of the women who volunteered to stay. She's excited and promised to treat Mma's daughter as a queen.

* * *

Eight days later, everybody in Amagwu gather in Ejike's hut for the name-giving ceremonies. Ejikeme being a wealthy farmer prepared hugely for the ceremony. This showed his excitement to welcome the damsel into his house. "I'm a father now," as he always says since after the day his wife gave birth. In traditions of the Igbo people, naming a child has always been a special event. This is because the name they give to a child sends a message each time they pronounce the name. The name bears a meaning and a history. Nwanyimma, who was to name the child, gave a great thought about the name she'll give her damsel. The elders started performing the rituals before naming the child. There are different groups of dancers in Ejike's compound that day. They came in their different outfits. The popular Agbomma dance group that hardly attends people's ceremony came for the naming ceremony. It started with ancestor recognition and divination. Elder Obiora poured wine libation to share the child's name with the ancestors. Nwanyimma dressed beautifully in her wrapper and blouse, and wore different colors of beads on her hands and necks. She rubbed white powder on her neck stood beside elder Obiora as he was performing the naming ceremony rituals. The old man looked at the baby, he told Mma to announce the name of the baby to the people that have gathered. She took a deep breath; she did not find it difficult trying to scratch her head to remember one. She already had a name in mind. With expression of excitement in her heart, she announced the name of the child to be "Anulika."

"*Oh*! Anulika *o...*" echoed the women there.

Mazi Ikeobi and his wife were seen coming in. Their four children were already there to eat and drink at the naming ceremony. They ordered them to eat and fill every space in their stomach because they'll not cook again. The wife tied nylon on her wrapper she planned to use and pack the leftovers. They came in and took a seat. Once Nwanyimma announced the child's name, Obiora carried the baby and presented her to the ancestors who told them to take care of her and make her flourish in all she does. The villagers chorused "*Ami o.*" He gave her back to her mother. She went and sat down with the child and the ceremony began fully. Each dance group performed but the Agbomma dance group caught every ones attention. They ate and drank to their satisfaction. Mazi Ikeobi was busy eating as if there was no tomorrow. His unkempt children were there behaving like him. They ate from group to group while the wife was avariciously packing the leftovers. Everybody that came to Ejike's child naming ceremony testified it to be the best they witnessed in Amagwu.

"If he could do this for a mere female child what'll he do for a male child? Kill a lion for him?" Mazi Ikeobi said while on their way home.

"Hum! I do not care, even if he wants to kill gorilla or chimpanzee. All I care now is this my food," said Mama Ifenyinwa smiling.

* * *

Two days later, the children were in Akpuato, they engaged in fight with a boy from the neighboring village. It's leisure time, the boy's sister Ihuoma caused the fight when she saw Akachi the third child of Mazi Ikeobi in a short with patches at the buttocks. She derided him as she could not hold her laughter. She's about seven years' old. She called pairs together to make jest of him, they mock and deride him singing in unison, "*Patch, patch ike mpu*"

"*Patch, patch ike mpu*"

They continued singing while out of frustration the child threw a stone at them. Unfortunately the stone hit Ihuoma who started the gibe. She burst out crying. His older brother who was about twelve ran and intervened. The children caused havoc in Akpuato that day, but they later succeeded in separating them. In the evening of that day, Ihuoma's mother brought her to Amagwu. She came to Amagwu and couldn't find Mazi Ikeobi's hut. Having walked into four huts, she found the hut with the description that suits that of Mazi Ikeobi's children. The woman confronted them to know why they have injured her child. Mazi Ikeobi and wife came out when they heard the thunderous voice of Ihuoma's mother. They inquired to know why she wanted to bring down their hut with her earthquake voice. She heard the cause of the problem, Mama Ihuoma who did not get to ask her daughter what occurred between her and Ikeobi' children pleaded for the insult, later she took her child home annoyed, and ranting that she will deal with her when they get home.

It was Orie day in Amagwu. At the fourth cockcrow, Ejikeme got up from his sleep. His wife and child were still asleep. He rolled out from the bed and stretched himself, yawning and took an old lantern, lit it as it was still dark. He went outside with the lantern, when he came out, he saw a myriad of birds perching from one tree to another. The birds fluttered around and chirped merrily while Ejikeme wished those birds could just shut up. The early morning wind blew in from the north, across the bosky narrow road. Ejikeme shivered and drew his clothe tighter around his neck and went closer to the *dogoyaro* tree (*Neem*), he broke the twig and used it as chewing stick. It is believed it helped to prevent tooth decay and gum disease. He brushed the stick up and down his mouth as he spit continuously. Soon enough, the sky started letting out light. He collected water from an earthen pot near the hut, rinsed his mouth, took the lantern, blew it out, and went inside. He got in. His wife was already awake while the child was still sleeping.

"*Oh*! *Nna anyi* I was even looking for you before you came in," Nwanyimma said.

"*Ah*! *Nkem*, have you forgotten that I told you I'll leave early to the farm today?" he asked.

"Oh no! I almost forgot. You ought to have woke me up to steam the food. At least, you eat before going," Nwanyimma said.

"*Nkem*, do not bother yourself, I can even steam the food myself. I do not want to take something before going because I'll soon be back that was why I woke early. He quickly put on his shorts and old white singlet. He took his machete and hoe, and hung it on his shoulder. As he was about to leave, he told his wife to take care of the child while he went off to the farm. His wife stood up and embraced him to say good-bye. He left to the farm as he sang and whistled.

* * *

Five years later, the baby girl Anulika grew elegantly and respectful. At that tender age, she was a paragon of beauty and started attending classes with other children at Akpuato when she became five. Nicole and Brandy were always amazed at the way she outsmarted her age mates. They both wished the clock would go back so to have ample time with Anulika; nurture her before they left Akpuato for the United States of America. It's unfortunate that they only had a year to complete their community service in Akpuato. Bravo to Nicole and Brandy. They're teachers every teacher should dream to be. Five years in Akpuato, they rehabilitated the community and those around. Except, Amagwu village, their children grew wild looking at their fathers and mothers gasconading that without them, every other village is footless. They go to classes with such attitude, always looking for trouble to buy. They're impudent children that are insignia of their parents. Our people will always say that the blacksmith who does not know how to forge a metal gong should look at the tail of a kite but Amagwu people did not know how to forge neither had they looked at the kite's tail. The children envied Anulika for her eagerness to learn. They hated her with passion. When she's five, Ifenyinwa the daughter of Mazi Ikeobi is fifteen. Chioye was thirteen, Akachi Eleven and Nnedi the last child was already ten years old. Mazi Ikeobi opted Ifenyinwa should learn how to make dress in her wife's sister shop.

"She isn't bright enough to have the formal education; she's a girl that will marry someday. She needs to have skilled work because no suitor wants a maiden without handwork," he included.

His wife isn't happy with the idea. She believed Ifenyinwa will pick up soon and she wouldn't want Anulika of yesterday to excel more than her own daughter. After much deliberation and negotiation she accepted that she go and learn dressmaking since she's fifteen.

"Soon suitors will eye her," she said. "She'll stop for now let us know if she'll catch up with skills first. If she learns it, she can start going with her brother's again to Akpuato. Perhaps, my intuition is telling me the formal education will turn out to be the best in the future," she said.

Her husband agreed with what she said.

On the Afo day, she took Ifenyinwa to her sister's shop at the Afo Amagwu, she told her to teach Ifenyinwa her niece how to make a dress.

"She's a woman and needed to have a handy work before suitors will start knocking," she said.

She accepted to take Ifenyinwa and teach her.

"If I do not teach her who else will I teach?" she said smiling.

She left Ifenyinwa there and told her to come back when the market closes. She entered the market and bought some food. They are lazy if you speak of farming. Although Amagwu is the center of farming in Igbo-etiti, Ikeobi and her husband have been lazy since they were a child. They were just learning to become left-handed in old age since they tried to work hard not to borrow from people.

* * *

One evening, at about six-twenty in the evening, Anulika was at the front porch of the hut cooking porridge with sand. Her mother was at the back of the hut trying to pack the palm kernel seed she spread on the sun during the day. No sooner than later, Ejikeme came from the bushy hut entrance, carrying his farm tools. The singlet he wore hung loose on his shoulder while he held the hoe and the machete in his hand. On his left, he held crickets he wrapped on the cocoyam leaf. He tied it round with palm fronds. When Anulika saw he approached the hut, she rose quickly to welcome him. Ejikeme dropped the farm tools and carried her. He inquired about her mother and she told him that she's at the back porch of the hut, trying to pack the palm kernel seeds. He gave her the cricket tied on a cocoyam leaf. She happily thanked her father and ran on her kneels as she called, "*Nne! Nne!*"

She got to her mother, showed her the present her father gave her, and she collected it from her. She came out from the back porch of the hut and greeted her husband who was still standing waiting for her. She brought a seat for her husband to sit down and then took the hoe and machete to the back porch of the hut and washed it.

She brought a seat and sat with her husband while they talked at a length. Later, she steamed the food, brought it out and they ate as happy family. They went to bed after they told their daughter stories about a tortoise. The story Anulika enjoyed the most was the one the tortoise went to the land of the spirits to look for his palm-kernel that fell there. The spirits presented him with a drum full of gifts because they have eaten the palm-kernel he came for. He went home broke the drum and different kinds of food started coming out from it. The tortoise and his household ate to their satisfaction. In few days, the food finished. Tortoise in his cunning nature this time threw another palm-kernel in the land of the spirit and went for it again. The spirit presented two drums for him to choose from. One of the drums was very big and the other was small. On his greedy nature, he chose the big drum without knowing it was filled with harmful insects of all kinds. Scorpions, snakes, frogs, mosquitoes, bed-bugs, to mention but few of the insects. He came home gather his household as usual and broke the drum. They got it hot from the insects' sting and bite that day.

Anulika was always happy each time she hears the story as she'll always say, 'that serves him right.'

* * *

The next day, the children gather at Akpuato as usual for their classes. During the class, Nicole and Brandy told them they will leave after one year. The teachers they raised will continue from where they stopped. Noise roared in the air as they shout in chide that they didn't want any other teacher than them. After much rioting by the pupils, Nicole and Brandy gave them many reasons they have to allow them to go. Anulika was unhappy because she hadn't spent time with them, and they are already going. Ikeobi's children were looking for such an opportunity. If they were to decide, they'd send them out before they could think of it. For them, everything about formal education is like bone on their throat. They have sworn never to come to Akpuato if the White Spirits should go. They decided to make up some stories they would tell their parents after that one year but one year turned into a decade in their eyes. They did not see reasons to why they partake in the so-called formal education they disliked.

After classes that day, every child went home. Anulika, five now was naturally intelligent, beautiful and bold, she waited behind. Amagwu has naively believed she must be a witch or devil's incarnate. They say she came from the White Spirits. She's articulate enough after a month she started the class with other children. What baffles them the more was her age. She sat with hands on her jaw as she sobbed. Nicole was arranging the instructional materials they used for the day. Suddenly, she saw her sitting alone when every other child had gone home. She approached her, sat beside her and inquired to know why she refused to go with the others. She held her face forward in a steady gaze at Nicole as tears trickled down her cheeks.

Nicole carried her on her laps, tried to clear the tears with the white handkerchief she held. She later demanded to know the village she came from. She told her she's from Amagwu.

"Amagu," replied Nicole,

Anulika nodded in affirmation. Nicole inquired to know if she knew her way home, she nodded she doesn't know. Bryan then came in and saw Nicole with the damsel crying. Nicole explained everything to him and told him that she has refused to go home while others were going. Brandy told Nicole that they have to take Anulika with them; maybe the parents will come looking for her, he said. They took her and left.

It was getting late; Ejikeme and his wife are yet to see their diamond, as they always call her. Nwanyimma could no longer hold herself, she cried that evening. Ejike tried all that he could to put her together by telling her that they'll find their daughter. They went to the huts of children in her class. They asked them about their daughter and where she is at. None of them knew.

When they got to Mazi Ikeobi's hut to ask their children, Mazi Ikeobi and the wife mocked them.

"Oh! We thought she's born with formal education in her head?" Mazi Ikeobi asked with a stellar smile.

"Isn't she wiser than the gods again? Why will she miss her way if she's intelligible enough as we think?" Asked mama Ifenyinwa who did not allow her children to come out and say anything.

Nwanyimma cried uncontrollably.

"She's only five years old, remember?" she said as she cried, "Why do you expect her to know everything?" she asked.

"Ah! Isn't she the epitome of formal education again?" Mama Ifenyinwa inquired as she laughed.

Ejike saw the conversation won't give them any clue related to where their child was, so he took his wife and left Ikeobi's hut angrily. Ikeobi and their wife went in jubilating and prayed they never see her.

At about seven-twenty in the evening, they came out from the hut, Nwanyimma and her husband decided to go to Akpuato that night to look for their only child. Our people say, "Bird at hand worth more than a thousand in the bush." The speed they walked was beyond the speed of sunlight. Nwanyimma was busy untying and retying her wrapper as she ran on her heels sobbing. If anybody has passed them on their way to Akpuato, I doubt they'll know. No sooner than later they got to Akpuato. They went to the village square where they normally have their class, but no child was there. Nwanyimma told her husband that they'll go to Okpalaugo's hut first because he'll have some information of where the teachers will be. Nicole, Brandy and Anulika had their dinner. They sat at the verandah of the hut talking. They inquired to know why she has been alone crying.

The girl looked at both, and said

"Teacher, it was barely some months I started classes with you. You both have influenced my life positively."

Surprisingly with their mouth opened to their jaw Nicole and Brandy shouted

"What?" How old are you?" They both echoed coincidentally.

"I'm five," said Anulika.

"Five years?" they shouted surprisingly.

"Nicole, wish we still have plenty of time to nurture this young and intelligent chap. I think she has a long way to go towards changing Africa," said Brandy with expression of excitement on his face.

"She's full of surprises; I'm shocked by the age and what she has," Nicole said.

Okpalaugo, Nwanyimma and Ejikeme came in and saw their daughter talking with the White Spirits. They took a long lasting breathe and thanked the gods. On seeing them, Anulika ran to her mother and embraced her. She carried her by the shoulder while Nicole and Brandy walked to them. Ejikeme thanked them for taking good care of their daughter. Brandy told them not to toil with Anulika's education. She'd make an incredible contribution towards Africa and its diaspora. They thanked them for having raised such a child. They took her to Okpalaugo's hut where they spent the night. Before the fifth cock crow, they went back to Amagwu village joyfully.

Chapter Eight

The sixth month of the year is planting season for Igboetiti people and planting season in all Africa. The first round of rain before planting takes place has fallen. The heaviness with which the rain fell that year in Igbo-etiti got all the farmers worried. They feared if they wronged the gods. Every nook and cranny of Igbo-etiti performed rituals to appeal the god of harvest before planting will take place. They feared planting that year because the way the sky opened its mouth and vomited the rain was a bell of warning. Obviously, they ran in thought of what the year after that year would look like if they did not plant that year. They would go hungry because they would have finished everything in their different barns. It rained heavily in Amagwu compared to other communities this got Ejike the wealthy farmer well-known in Amagwu worried. They finished appealing the gods with blood of goats, fowls and bounty of crops from their previous harvest. The chief priest ordered them to go on, till the earth and plant their crops; the god of farming will protect the farms.

Ejike and other wealthy farmers hired laborers to help them clear their farms, till and cultivate on them.

Six month, Bryan and Nicole were also rounding off to go back to United States of America. It's their last day with the children in Akpuato. They told them a day before that will have their teachers selected. In truth, there are maidens and few mothers who showed interest on the Western education brought to Akpuato through Nicolas and Wiggins intervention. Male chaps showed less interest because they're always out of the village to farm. It was a way to help their families in daily ends meet. Brandy and Nicole selected four maidens and two mothers with a male who was about twenty-two years old to place the students into Nursery, Primary and Secondary according to one's understanding. They selected them based on results from their previous academic performances. This marked the history of education in Africa. They placed Anulika in primary one. Ikeobi's children were in primary one with her. Age wasn't a priority Brandy and Nicole used. They did it that way because they have low understanding and poor attitude to formal education. There are older chaps placed in primary one. Anulika was the youngest child among them. When Chioye and his two siblings got home, they complained to their mother and father how the White Spirits stupidly put them and Anulika in the same class after the selection. Their parents were unhappy and told them their enemies are doing it, so they'll stop you from acquiring formal knowledge. They promised them that with time, when the White Spirits have gone, they must go to Akpuato to change their class.

"How on earth will they place you in the same class with the child you saw her pregnancy?" Mama Ifenyinwa said.

The children were happy getting a positive response from their parents. Anulika on getting home announced the good news to her mother and father who sat under the mango tree at the verandah of the hut talking and taking garden egg. They were happy and encouraged her to keep it up. You are going to one day lead the world into formal education, they said.

One week later, Nicole and Brandy held a week intensive class for the seven teachers selected to represent them. They specially involved Anulika to the lesson because they believed they saw a future in her yet to uncover and nurture. They told the teachers to take good care of Anulika, they taught them class manners, how to write different names, prepare a result sheet to encourage competition among the students. This marked the era of issuing result to students in Africa. After the one-week intensive lesson, Nicole and Brandy presented a wrist watch to Anulika.

"As this watch ticks, you should know that no time is a waste. Use every minute you've to make an incredible discovery that'll help you change the world. Keep in mind time and tide waits for no one," Nicole said as she handed the gold wristwatch to her. Nicole and Brandy embraced her. It's their last day in Akpuato before they boarded a jet sent by the United States Government to pick them up in Akpuato early in the next day. Anulika raised a pale skinned hand at both of them for a last good-bye as tears trickled down her cheeks. Nicole and Brandy held her as they both cried with her.

In the evening of that day, Mazi Ikeobi decided to pay a visit to his brother. At the door mouth he started shouting, "Anybody home?"

Ejikeme who was inside his hut resting told him to come inside. Mazi instead asked him to bring a chair outside for them to have a brother to brother talk. Ejikeme knew well the brother to brother talk could only mean something he wouldn't embrace. It's either his brother has found another fault or has come to quarrel him to leave the land at Onuiyi. He knew it belonged to him but out of greedy the lazy, Ikeobi wouldn't allow him to drink and keep the cup. Respectfully, he brought out a bench raised his voice to call his wife. She's at the back porch of the hut getting ready to prepare dinner for the family. They sat down while Nwanyimma came out to answer her husband's call. On seeing Mazi Ikeobi she greeted but he responded sluggishly. Ejikeme told his wife to get a kola nut on his bag that he hung on the wall. She brought the kola nut from the brown bag hung on the wall washed it and placed it on an earthen plate, and brought it to her husband. She squatted and gave the kola nut to her husband and left the two brothers to iron their matters privately. He presented the kola nut to Mazi Ikeobi, but he told him to pray over the kola nut and break it.

"*Onye abiala beya na-awa oji,*" said Ikeobi.

Ejike took the kola nut, raised it, and thanked the gods and their ancestors. Mazi Ikeobi continued saying "*Amin o,*" as he prayed over the kola nut.

When he finished blessing the kola nut, he broke it and then put the four pieces on the earthen plate.

"*Okwa ahia ano ndi Amagwu*, Eke, Orie, Afo na Nkwo," said Ejike as he presented the plate to his brother to take the kola.

They started eating the kola nut. Ikeobi waited, cleared his throat in wholesome nature.

"Ejike! Ejike! Ejike!" He called. "How many times did I call you?" asked Ikeobi.

Ejike answered him, "Three times of course, what's the problem?" he inquired.

Ikeobi looked at him and nodded in dismay, and continued, "What an elder sat down and saw, if a child climbs the highest mountain in Akpuato, he won't see it."

"Brother you still speak in riddles. Why don't you go straight to the point and stop beating about the bush?" Ejikeme said.

Mazi Ikeobi shook his head with expression of surprise and disappointment for his brother's poor understanding, and cleared his throat again,

"*Ahem,* you know that you are my only brother. I'll never do anything that's not for benefit of us. Brother, it just the two of us left out of the ten children our mothers gave birth to. Others are still-birth, or they died before they were of age," Ikeobi said. He paused and gave a bite on the kola with his front teeth, then said, "It's true papa married your mother when my mother couldn't bear again after six deliveries with one alive. You're the only child left after 4 attempts. I'm here to tell you to stand on your feet and think like a man of integrity we know you to be." He was still speaking when Ejike caught in,

"Brother, I still don't understand this history of yours."

Ikeobi became annoyed; he thought his younger brother was playing with his intelligence and decided to be plain enough by telling him he needed to marry another maiden, a wife who'll bore him a male child, one to inherit his name and property.

"What do you want this place to become when you die, and your child marries? Bush, forest or desert?" he asked angrily. "Supposing our father gave birth to only female children what do you think would become of his two homes? My brother you're son of the soil, farmer well-known in Amagwu your fatherland."

Ejikeme became infuriated. First, it was marry another wife to bear you a child. His wife has given birth to a child, the whole dance changed to a male child.

"Brother, thank you but I think I'm not complaining. I'm happy with my family boy or girl, I do not care," he said angrily.

"*Tufiakwa!* May the gods forgive you," Ikeobi said. "Ejike, if only you know the dangers behind having a mere girl as your only child, you'll listen and obey what I'm telling you."

This time, Ejike got up and told him when he's done taking the kola nut; he knew the path to his hut. He left with expression of anger on his face. Mazi Ikeobi was aghast when his younger brother left him; he stood up and left in anger. When Ejikeme got in, his wife seeing him moody inquired to know why her husband was unhappy after talking with his brother. He told her that he was alright and promised not to do anything to hurt her and their only child and embraced her.

Since it's time for planting, mama Ifenyinwa pleaded with her husband for them to be involved in planting so they won't buy nor beg people for credit the next year. Mazi Ikeobi agreed with his wife and told her they won't go to people for food items next year. Perhaps, they need to learn how to become left-handed at old age.

The people of Igbo-etiti had cleared, tilled and planted the varieties of crops for the year, expecting good harvest months after. It was Nkwo day. It was a dark and stormy night. Amagwu people were sound asleep as a heavy downpour came that night. The rain fell in torrents as every river overflew its banks. It's unfortunate for people of Amagwu that live in a hilly setting; their farmland flooded leaving behind no crop for the people. The disaster was unbearable. It affected the Amagwu people because they planted every crop in the barn .Except for few they left to eat until the next harvest.

That year, Amagwu people were in a great famine, including Ejikeme the great farmer of Amagwu. Indeed, it's hard time for them. They needed a solution to end the famine before it became worst. The people of Amagwu well-known for farming in Igbo-etiti started going to the neighboring villages. They went to work for other people for pay and food.

They thanked the gods that the flood didn't affect those villages. If it had affected them, the whole people of Igbo-etiti would have starved to death. Amagwu children above the age of ten worked in the villages around them. Ejikeme told his wife he would never allow her and his only daughter to do the same. It annoyed him each time he thought of the drought. He never wanted his only child to suffer but the condition was beyond his reach. He vowed to work hard to restore his barn in order before the next planting season. Indeed, he always worked with the strength of four men put together. Few months later, Ejikeme started working in other people's farm. He fulfilled his promise of restoring his barn for the next planting season.

* * *

One afternoon, Nwanyimma was in the hut sleeping with her daughter when she had a dream. She woke up suddenly with her brown face covered with sweat. She had been dreaming a bad dream, and suddenly her bright dark eyes flew open. She spiked her pitch-black hair, wondering what the dream meant. She got up and ran to the room where her husband sat on a reclining chair leaning his head backward. Seeing him, she took a brief breathe and murmured,

"Oh! Thank the gods it was a dream, she brought a chair, sat beside her husband who hardly noticed her presence. She took a lasting gaze at him and decided not to wake him up but later made up her mind to tell him about dream when he's up. Nwanyimma was so worried about the dream for her husband and friends were going to clear the bush for one of them as they normally do for one another during planting seasons. People of Amagwu were all ready to plant on their farms for the next planting season. They already started clearing the bush waiting for the first rainfall.

At seven O'clock in the morning, Ejikeme got ready to go to work on Ikemba's farm that day because it was his turn. He wore his old short and singlet as usual and was about to go when his wife hurriedly came to him with expression of fear and depression on her face. He inquired to know why she was moody. The wife told him she wouldn't want him out of her sight that day.

"*Nkem* why? You know I have to go because tomorrow they'll work on our farm," he said.

"I know but still I don't want you out my sight today," Nwanyimma insisted.

Ejike drew her closer and said, "Please *Nkem* allow me to go. I promise I'll be at home to attend to you and Anulika's needs tomorrow."

She frowned her face, "Nkem, I had a bad dream yesterday when I was sleeping but never wanted to disturb your sleep when I woke up," she said. "Dream?" he asked. "What's the dream about?" He inquired.

"In my dream, I saw you fall from a tall tree and when you fell from there, you lied unconsciously, and this made me wake up suddenly.

Ejike smiled.

"Palm tree?" He asked.

He calmed her by telling her it was just a dream and sometimes dreams turn out not to be real. He included. "Nevertheless, I'm not a palm wine tapper," he said laughing.

His wife was still not ready to let him go to the work that day.

"You know if I didn't go to help them, they'll not come for my own tomorrow. Please *Nkem* allow me to go," he pleaded.

The wife later accepted but advised him to take good care of himself. He embraced his wife and she waved to say good-bye while he was leaving. Worry was still written boldly on her face. She prayed for the gods to protect her husband.

In the farm, the four friends of Ejikeme waited for him to arrive so they start the work. The four friends include: Ikemba whose farm they are to clear that day, he is of average height, plump, dark skinned and in his early forties; Nwafor was short and squat with raven black hair and is in his late forties; Ndudi is tall and slim with a round face and fair in complexion; Emenike, the youngest among them is petite and in his late thirties. They sat under a palm tree and talked. They were worried about Ejikeme as he is rarely late to work.

"It's better we share the work and start working, we're not sure Ejike will be here today. He has never been this late since we started working together as friends," Ndudi said.

They had a prolonged negotiation whether to share the work and start or wait for him to arrive.

"We know the best time for working is in the morning when the sun is not scorching," Ndudi said again.

"Yes, we know but at least let us wait for him for some time please," Nwafor snapped.

They were still arguing when they saw him coming.

"Oh! Here he comes," Emenike said.

They held their head forward as they looked at him coming. When he approached them, he pleaded for coming late. They accepted his apology and shared the work as discussed.

"Ejike! Ikemba called.

"*Oo*!" he replied.

He reminded him of the palm wine he had at his house yesterday and later inquired to know where he bought it from.

"It's from Ekpof village when I went for work there; they said the man was the best palm wine tapper in their village. After work that day, they took me to his house and I decided to buy a few bottles from him because I was not with enough money," Ejike said.

"*Ee*! I believe he's the best even in Amagwu, he's beyond comparison," Ikemba said. Interested to know if the palm wine remains he'll visit again. When he told him it has finished, Ikemba then told him he'll take him to Ekpof, so they'll buy some more. Nwafor interrupted them, "Why are you men negotiating on what you'll do this evening when you still have plenty of work to do here?" he said smiling.

"Nwafor dear, if you can taste this palm wine, you'll know the difference.

If you take that one with Nwanyi Ukwunnu's pepper soup, at night you'll be strong enough to do the work. It is an energy booster my dear," Ikemba said laughing.

"Ikemba, you're too much *o*," Emenike said laughing back.

Soonest, it was as god of silent passed they all kept quiet as they worked.

When it was time for a short break, they went and sat down talking and also drank water. No sooner than later Ejikeme quickly got up on the floor shouting,

"Snake! Snake! Snake!"

His co-workers ran to his rescue he was only pointing to the spot the snake took as he continued shouting snake! Snake! Ikemba tried spotting the snake but it was nowhere around. As they were still looking for the snake, Ejikeme fell down and lay unconsciously. It was a dark snake that bites him. Snakes are believed by the tradition of Igbo-etiti people when it bites you, you'll die within a few hours of bite. Tradition believes a snake bites people that committed an abominable act. They decided to stop the work and take their friend home.

Nwanyimma took a molded plate, put some pepper she wanted to sundry in it and was about to put it on the lower roof of her hut when suddenly she fell off the roof and injured her leg. She ran in thought if something bad had happened to her husband as reviewed by the bad dream she had. She paced round with her hands on her head as she prayed for the gods to guide her husband. She was still pacing round the compound when she saw the men carrying her husband home. She ran to them to know what has happened to him. The men asked for mat to lay him on it. She ran in and brought a mat, Ejikeme lay on the mat unconsciously. His daughter sat beside him crying. Nwanyimma gave out a shrill cry which sent the villagers to their hut. Mazi Ikeobi and his wife also came to know what brought about the shout cry in his brother's compound. When he saw his only brother lying breathlessly on the mat, he demanded to know what had happened to him. They sent Emenike who could ran faster than the others to go and fetch Mazi Ikemefuna, medicine man in Amagwu who specialized on all kinds of snake bites. They believed the leaves, shrubs, twigs and roots of plants were his friends. Amagwu people said at midnight he interacts with those plant parts, each of them tells him the sickness it cures. Emenike came in with the old man with grey hair. Ikemefuna walked in with an old stick and bag that hung on his right shoulder, the bag contained his medicinal items. When he approached Ejikeme, he ordered the men to take him inside. They took him in, and he told them to leave while he attends to him alone. Nwanyimma was crying uncontrollably while the women tried to put her together. The condition of Ejike didn't move mama Ifenyinwa one bit. Mazi Ikemefuna washed the wound, and invited his ancestors to come and intervene. He brought a kola nut from his bag, and said some incantations, broke it in pieces and threw them on the floor for his ancestors. When he looked at the wounds again, he shook his head expressing he won't work on Ejike's wound since he believed he committed an abominable act. He took in the medicine items he brought out went out where the people gathered. Seeing him, Nwanyimma ran to him, "*Nna anyi* please tell me you revived my husband," she said to him.

Mazi Ikemefuna looked at her, and at the crowd that gathered, he shook his head again and said "Woman, it was so unfortunate a black snake bite your husband."

"*Aru*!" the people echoed but some of the villagers were kind enough. They sympathized with Nwanyimma with much shaking of head.

Mazi Ikemefuna left the compound while Nwanyimma ran inside with her daughter to see her husband. Before she could go in, her husband gave up the ghost. She cried bitterly with her daughter, dark reality she didn't believe trapped her. In a flash, she saw her life before her. Ikeobi pointed accusing fingers at her saying his only brother died trying to protect his evil wife. He ordered that his brother's corpse is thrown to the evil forest. The young men wrapped Ejike's corpse on a mat, carried him to the evil forest led by the elders. Nwanyimma with her daughter cried bitterly, she could only say,

"Where'll I go from here? Ejike what do you want me to do? *Eeh*! Ewo! It's finished *o*...!"

* * *

Three months later, Nwanyimma was with her daughter cooking in her kitchen when Mazi Ikeobi came in with his wife. On seeing them, Nwanyimma greeted but Ikeobi told her angrily they've not come for greetings. He reminded her that having a girl as ones only child in Amagwu remained the same as barren.

"Now your husband is dead, I'm the man of the house now.

I've come to claim my brother's properties," he included.

"*Ah*! Mazi, have you come to mock me? It's barely three months my husband died and here you are for his property,"

Nwanyimma said angrily, "If I may ask, which property?"

Ikeobi and the wife became annoyed. Ikeobi told her everything left by his late brother is rightfully his according to the tradition and told her he has come for them but will wait to follow the traditional orders. First, on the next market day, they'll both see the elders, so they'll explain the culture well to her if she has forgotten. "Maybe she's still crept with mourning, he said mockingly.

"Mama Ifi lets go," said Ikeobi.

They both left the house while Nwanyimma and her daughter stood gazing as tears prickled down their cheeks. They got to the unjust elders the next day who told Nwanyimma to hand everything over to her husband's brother. They told her tradition must be obeyed. She obeyed the elders and did as they said because she has no choice. Life became tough for her and her daughter. Nwanyimma believed that if the yam used in sacrifice does not die prematurely, it will eventually germinate. It'll only take time for that to happen.

Chapter Nine

Six years later, the United States Government in collaboration with other foreign state governments had come to Africa to develop the continent. The coalition-built schools including nurseries, primary, secondary and tertiary institutions. They first built the University of Ibadan. The Nigerian Government became a strong initiative. Development had reached all of Nigeria. Thirty-six states created and everybody lived as the whites. The mode of dressing changed, religion started emanating from traditional religion to Christianity. Amagwu also travelled to the city because they believed life in city to be easier compared to life in the village. Nwanyimma and the child were still in Amagwu village because there was no one to take them to the city. Amagwu had their own Nursery, primary and community secondary schools by the help of the Enugu State government. Anulika was twelve years old when she wrote her Common Entrance Examination. She waited for her results. This intelligent and paragon of beauty became the talk of youths at twelve. Each time she passes by, they strain their neck starring at her beauty. Within a mouth, five suitors came asking for Anulika's hand in marriage. Her mother refused saying she was still tender for marriage. Even though Anulika's mother accepted to give her out for marriage to one of those suitors, she wouldn't agree. She already told her mother she must finish her education up to the University level. She agreed to see to her educational needs no matter how tough and ugly their condition may become.

* **

One month later, Udoka came from the town to seek for Ifenyinwa's hand in Marriage. At first, her mother wanted a rich suitor for her, but they were not coming. When Udoka came to their house for the first introduction with two elders from his family, Mazi Ikeobi inquired to know if her daughter in question was aware or whether he had had a formal discussion with his daughter. He isn't the one marrying. Udoka told him they've talked it over with one another. They presented the wine they brought. Mazi Ikeobi offered them kola nut and they talked as they were taking the nut. Mazi Ikeobi inquired of where he's staying in the town and his means of livelihood. He told him he's staying in Enugu town and he's a car mechanic by profession.

"A mechanic?" asked Mazi Ikeobi, "Oh! That's good, at least there's lot of cars in Nigeria this time."

For him, a mechanic marrying his first daughter sucks, but it was the only way she could leave the village he thought. Ifenyinwa came in and greeted the elders. When she got to where they sat, her suitor and his relatives surveyed her young body with expert eyes as if to assure themselves that she was beautiful and ripe. She sat beside her mother while her father told her Udoka has come to officially announce his interest in marrying her. He later asked her if she knows him and would want to marry him. Ifenyinwa looked at Udoka and smiled, and agreed she'll marry him. The families were happy. Udoka told them they'll be coming back in the next two market days to perform the marriage rights. They presented a marriage list to them to get items ready. They stood up to leave while Ikeobi and his wife saw them off and went back to the house. Mama Ifenyinwa became excited as her daughter is to marry a man in the city that has handy work. Since her daughter knows how to make a dress, he'll help her open a shop where she'll be sewing. Secondly, she'll also take his younger brother Chioye to stay with them while he learns the mechanic business, she thought.

• **

One week later, Udoka and Ifenyinwa traditionally had gotten married and left for Enugu town with Chioye who the father advised to be obedient. He never agreed for once that Ifenyinwa is older than him. His mother told him his sister is now the madam of the house and he was going to live in the town. When they got to Enugu town, Ifenyinwa and his brother were acting naively while walking down the street. They stood for minutes watching objects that caught their eyes. Udoka walked at the front, and stopped to call their attention before they get lost in the street of Enugu. They got to Udoka's house; it was a public yard in Abakpa. He occupied two rooms; one of the rooms was his parlor. It has three cushions and three side chairs in it and a 14-inch colored television. At the window side stood a standing fan. They came in and they took a brief breathe of relief *huff*. Ifenyinwa sat on the three in one cushion as she took a steady gaze at the television. Chioye dropped his bag and sat beside his sister. Udoka went to the other room which he used as bed room to dust and arrange it before he'll take his wife there. Soon enough, he finished arranging the room; he came into the sitting room and called his wife. He took her to the bedroom and showed her where to keep her belongings. They later showered, ate and went to the sitting room to watch television.

They were amazed by the images on the television screen. They never see one in Amagwu though some of the rich families in Amagwu had television, but they lived an isolated life. He taught them how to control the television.

* **

One month later, the common entrance examination result came out. Anulika scored above other students in Igbo-etiti. She was posted to Amagwu Community Secondary School. It was a popular community secondary school that attracted student from all over. This is because they have high quality teaching staff sent to the school by Enugu state government. The academic performance of students in Amagwu community secondary school was impressive. The only school in Igboetiti that had tried to outshine them was the school they named after Nicolas and Bryan, the two men from the United States of America that came to Africa. During inter-schools competition, it was always a tug-of-war when Community Secondary School Amagwu and Nico-Bryan Secondary School came across. Then, Akachi had written his junior certificate examination. He was waiting for the result to know if he'll advance to the senior class. Though his parents told him that if for any reason the Junior WAEC came out and he failed, they'll take him to Onitsha to learn trade.

Nnedi their last daughter wasn't bright, but they had promised her she must read to the university level. So they boast of her as the graduate out of the four children. She was to enter J.S.S.3 when school resumes.

It was Monday morning; Nwanyimma has bought everything needed for her daughter to start school. She did not buy school uniforms because she was unaware of the school the government would post her to. She neatly dressed on her gown and set early to school. It excited her because it was her first day in college. All the students of Community Secondary School in Amagwu were looking sparkling in their blue and white school uniforms. It was about eight in the morning when the senior prefect Ezenyelu Chikwado finished conducting the assembly and stepped aside for the principal's welcome speech for the New Academic session. Dr. Iwu Anyanwu was the principal of Community Secondary School Amagwu dressed in a black trouser, and a white shirt that has blue stripes. The jacket he wore over his broad shoulders had neatly polished buttons. He was wearing glasses with alertness in his eyes behind the glasses that sat crookedly on his nose. Dr. Iwu is short and thick. Despite what he lacked by the way of height, he commands too much respect from the students and teachers at large. It was told that Dr. Iwu was a non-nonsense man. He deals with issues as they came without procrastination. He was not a man of too many words but of action. When he came up to the stage, he looked at the students through his glasses. There must be about five thousand students that filed according their classes. The crowd was too much that if one threw a grain of sand up, it will not find its way to the earth again. He looked to every corner, shook his head and started his speech;

"Dear teachers and students good morning! Welcome back. I'd like to especially welcome the newly admitted students who have just joined us. We welcome you to Community Secondary School Amagwu, a great citadel of learning. I want to gladly tell you the school still stands out and has no comparison both morally, and academically. I can see you in a high spirit, dressed up neatly in school uniform, though I know good number of you are yet to get theirs. I'm sure that you'll enjoy your studies and school life. I want to also use this medium to welcome our returning students. My best wishes to you. I pray for the academic year to be rewarding."

The students echoed, "Amen!"

"Now, I want to gladly announce to us the best student in the recently released common entrance examination is here in Community Secondary School Amagwu. If she's here I want her to come up to the stage so you can see her."

Anulika was shy as she covered her face with her left hand and climbed up the stairs. The students started murmuring, the principal yelled at them to keep quiet. She came up, introduced herself as Miss Udemba Anulika. She got the principal and teachers handshakes. The principal encouraged her to put in more effort because Community Secondary School will always be ready to give her the best. He then ended by telling all the students to be of high moral standards.

"Do the right, and do the right," he said and told them to match to their classes.

Nnedi, Ikeobi's daughter was to repeat a class in Community Secondary School because she failed woefully; she has to repeat J.S.S 2.

"If she fails again, she'll look for another school for unserious students. We don't raise academic morons and weaklings," said the principal.

She became envious of Anulika the best student announced and promised to make her stay in the school a living hell for her.

• * *

Two week later, Akachi's result came out and unfortunately, he performed too badly. His father arranged for his wife's brother in Onitsha to take Akachi with him, so he'll go and learn trade while Nnedi continued with her education. She never told her parents the teachers told her to repeat class.

• * *

One Tuesday morning, Anulika was going to school in her sparkling school uniform. It was her first day of wearing the school uniform because her mother just sewed it newly. She was walking on the bosky road when suddenly she met with Nnedi and her lazy colleagues. They stopped her, told her to lay and roll on the dusty floor with her school uniform that looked as snow. She had no choice than to follow their instructions. They bullied her and ordered her to not to tell anyone what they did. She stood up crying, kept going to school not minding the state of her school uniform. She got to school, her form teacher inquired to know what happened. She hid the truth from her as instructed by the naughty students that bullied her.

* **

Two years later, Anulika was in J.S.S 3 getting ready for her Junior Secondary School examination. Nnedi managed to enter S.S.1 by cheating in examinations because she has decided to study up to the university level, not minding cheating till she gets there.

It was on Tuesday morning, Anulika was getting ready to go to school but her mother lay unconsciously on the bed deteriorating in health. She didn't want to tell her daughter she was sick. She never wanted anything to bother her at school. When she got ready for school, she went to the room where her mother was.

"It was unlike my mother sleeping when I'm about to go school," she said worriedly. When she got in, Mma's condition has gotten worse. She decided to stop school that day and look after her mother who was down with sickness. At first, she decided to write a letter to her teacher that she won't be coming to school that day because she has to stay back and look after her sick mother. She took the letter to Nnedi to help her deliver it to her class teacher. She accepted to give the letter to the teacher as soon as she gets to school. Anulika went to the medicine man to come and help her mother regain her health. Ezego examined Nwanyimma, he found out her condition has gone beyond herbal medicine reach. He told Anulika her mother has to go to the hospital in the city, "Otherwise she'll die of the sickness," he said and went out.

Anulika promised her mother she'll seek help from her uncle to go to the hospital in the city.

"If they've not collected everything from us, I'd sell some items; raise money for your hospital bill," she said expressing worry on her face.

Her mother with a low voice told her that uncle will never accept to give the help she seeks.

"I'm his worst enemy since I married his brother. Perhaps, he would prefer my death," she said as she coughed continuously.

Anulika won't hold the sight of seeing her mother lying helplessly ran to Mazi Ikeobi's hut, on getting there, he sat on a reclining chair on his *obi*. His wife sat on a small wooden chair, her wrapper about to touch the ground. The flat wooden chair has a calabash of garden eggs in it. They were both having a good time eating the garden eggs as they discuss.

Soon, Anulika arrived, greeted them as she stood with her arms by the side. With voice like a foghorn, Mazi Ikeobi inquired to know what brought her to their house. She hardly comes except when her shadow is chasing her, he said. She spoke in a brittle voice and told them her mother was sick and needs urgent medical attention.

"*Ehe*! If she needs medical attention, is this a hospital that you have come?" Mama Ifenyinwa asked.

Anulika told them that she needs their assistance to take her mother to the hospital in the city.

"City?" Mazi Ikeobi inquired, "Do you think I'm Diamond bank, Access bank or Fidelity bank?" He asked with anger on his face.

"None," said his wife.

"I want you now to go back to your witch mother, tell her that she is receiving her pay for killing my only brother," Ikeobi said.

Anulika knelt down and pleaded with him to help them that her mother will pay back when she regains her health. Mama Ifi yelled at her and told her to take their message back to her sick mother. She left the house crying, thinking of whom to go to but seemed nothing came to her mind. She later made up her mind to call back the medicine man as she believed she'll respond and soon get better. He offered them the help without collecting any pay, but he told her the herbs may not help her mother get better since her condition has aggravated beyond herbs.

* * *

One week later, it seemed she was not getting better, it worsened every day. Her eyes clouded with months of pain, obstructed by the thinning hair. Her clothes hung loosely around her skeletal figure, and her skin was paler than the full moon outside. Anulika cried bitterly as she watched her mother die slowly, she decided to go back to her uncle, "May be this time he'll have a change of heart," she said. She got to Ikeobi's hut, and received same answer from them again."

It was on Eke day when Amagwu people were free from farming. It was a sunny afternoon; Nwanyimma suddenly gave up the ghost. Anulika got into the hut to check on her mother. She noticed she has ceased breathing, went closer to clear her doubts because for her it was like a nightmare. She raised her hands, listened to her heart beat but she lied breathlessly. She ran out of the hut, gave a shrill cry that sent the villagers to their hut. She cried uncontrollably with the crazy thoughts of joining her mother because she thought there was nothing else left for her. Mazi Ikeobi ordered the young chaps to take her body to the evil forest because that was what she deserved since she had no male child. Anulika tried to stop them from taking her mother's corpse to the evil forest but they pushed her aside. She wept bitterly while mama Ezekwesiri and other women around tried to put her together. Mama Eze promised to be a mother to her. It looked like the end of the world for her. She thought of why her mother left her in the hands of those who never loved her.

"These beautiful dreams you've for me mother, where are you now ?" she asked continuously with a furry mournful voice that took the high notes in a prolonged painful squeal.

Chapter Ten

The grief that accompanies early loss of a mother can ebb and flow through a daughter's life. Some months after the death of Anulika's mother, her uncle decided to take Anulika to stay with them since she was still too young to take care of her needs. First the wife thought of how helpful she would be to them in the farm and in doing home chores. When they brought her, they told her vividly she cannot continue with her education since they won't afford to pay for her school fees and that of their daughter as well. She accepted because she had no choice.

It was a Wednesday; Anulika was still sleeping, it was seventwenty in the morning , mama Ifi got to where she laid covering herself with a piece of wrapper and yelled at her to wake up. Get ready, go to the farm. She added. She stood up and greeted her. She was angry Anulika overslept.

"Do you sleep like this in your paternal home when they were alive?" She said angrily.

Anulika apologized for waking up late. Nnedi had already gone to school while she told the poor orphan to get up and dress to the farm. She ordered her to harvest all the cocoyam in the farm and raise the yams that fell off their ridges accordingly before coming back. When she was about to go, she asked for her food but instead got a shout. She took a basket; machete and a hole. She balanced the basket on her head and left for the farm. On her way to the farm, she met many students of Community Secondary School Amagwu going to school. Some of the students insulted and humiliated her. Some pitied her for her condition "Oh! What an intelligent student," said one of the students.

"Oh yes! She is one of the best students in Community Secondary School," said the second girl, "have you forgotten how she won all the prizes in every subject during the last prize giving day?" She included.

Anulika overheard the students talking about her, started crying as she was going to the farm.

* * *

One early morning, she was coming back from the stream; wore a gown and carried brimming water pail on her head with her left hand placed on the pail; she walked for a few metres away from the stream and met with Emeka. Emeka is tall, dark and average body built, probably in his early thirties. He is a well-known businessman in the Amagwu village, a man every mother would like her daughter to marry. He had come home in search of a wife as they always believe that when you reach the age of marriage, you go for village girls because they are the wife material. For one week he was home, his mother has shown him five different girls, but he rejected them. Seeing Anulika, he shouted he has seen the girl he has been looking for. At first, he decided not to talk to her but to follow her without her consent to know where she was coming from. When Anulika approached him, she greeted respectfully. Insatiable Emeka melted down when he heard her angelic voice.

"Hello dear, how are you?" He asked excitedly.

"I'm fine, thank you?" She answered.

She kept walking home while Emeka followed her. When she got to the hut entrance, she entered and helped herself put down the pail while Emeka stood at a distance stretching his neck to see her. He later went home and told his mother he has seen a girl he would want to marry and demanded the marriage right performed immediately so he'll go back to the city. The mother inquired to know if he has officially informed the girl in question, he nodded in disagreement and told her he hasn't. She told him to see the girl privately. It's done before seeing the bride's parents. Emeka bluntly refused saying that no girl in Amagwu will dare refuse him not even when he has displayed his riches.

* * *

One evening, mama Ifenyinwa was in the kitchen in front porch of her hut cooking. Her husband sat on a reclining chair under the African pear tree. Anulika had gone to the stream as usual while Nnedi was helping her mother at the kitchen. Emeka came in with her mother with two elders. He held a fancy yellow nylon that looked new. Inside the nylon was two bottles of red wine which they brought for the first visit to the in-law's house. When they came in, they went to Mazi Ikeobi and they exchanged pleasantries. Mazi Ikeobi welcomed them and signaled his daughter to get seat for their visitors. When Emeka's mother saw Nnedi, she whispered to her son if Nnedi was the one, but he nodded in disagreement. They sat down "*Nnonuo!*" said mazi Ikeobi again.

"*Ehe!*" replied the elders.

He signaled his wife to get kola nut for them. She brought the kolanut and handed it to her husband, took a seat beside him with smiles on her face. They thanked the gods, broke the kola nut and talked as they ate nut. One of the elders cleared his throat in wholesome nature

"Ahem," and said, "Mazi, our people say what a hen looks for when it rains is special to her."

"*Obu eziokwu*," they echoed uniformly.

He continued,

"Our son here," pointing at Emeka, "has seen the bone of his bone in this house. We come to inform you we'll be coming in next three market days to perform the marriage rites."

He brought the wines and kept it on a chair near Mazi Ikeobi. "We brought this wine for our first visit."

Mazi Ikeobi was happy though not aware of the person they were referring to. He thought it would be his daughter. Mama Ifi sat expressing happiness on her face because Emeka is a man every woman would want to be his mother in-law. Mazi Ikeobi inquired to know if their daughter was aware of his intentions. Emeka told them they're yet to have private discussion but he knew the girl will love him the way he loved her. They laughed over it because when money speaks, men obey. Mazi Ikeobi told his wife to go and tell her daughter that her husband and his people have come. She was about getting up when suddenly they saw Anulika coming with a pail of water balanced on her head.

"Here she comes," said Emeka pointing at her.

With their mouth opened to their jaw, Ikeobi and the wife shouted surprisingly, "What?"

"Anulika is only fourteen," said Ikeobi.

"I know, but she's the one that has won my love since the first day I saw her," Emeka admitted.

They pleaded with him to marry Nnedi instead and leave Anulika. They weren't considering Anulika's tender age for marriage. They wanted Emeka to marry their daughter instead because they believed he's a wealthy businessman who owns two cars and lives in a big house in the city. They thought of the good life he'll give their daughter and them as well. They decided to call Anulika to come and welcome her husband and his people. Mama Ifi had arcanely(check) warned her to disagree with the proposal when she gets there. She never knew that Anulika was not even ready for marriage at that age. She only gave her reasons to say no to the proposal because that was what she should've done. When Anulika came, she greeted them and stood with opens arms. Emeka astonished and deeply hurt when Anulika turned down the proposal.

"I'm not ready for marriage," Anulika said. "I'm not ready now. I need to discover myself, my future before marriage," she added.

"Please do marry me Anulika," said Emeka. "I'll help you discover those dreams of yours," he said worriedly.

"Please sir, do understand me, I'm not ready and I'm not going to marry you, I'm only but fourteen" she said and left angrily.

Mazi Ikeobi and the wife became excited. They presented their daughter Nnedi and told him to marry her instead since her sister refused. Emeka got up quickly with rage that boiled in his body left without talking. His mother and the other elders left with him. Mazi Ikeobi was uncontrollably angry.

* * *

One early morning, Mama Ezekwesiri decided to go to Ikeobi's hut to see how her friend's daughter is fairing. She brought with her two yams, watermelon and groundnuts, when she came in, there was nobody in the hut; she put down the basket she carried and went to the back porch of the hut as she kept shouting, "*Onye noo nso.*"

She was about to go when she saw mama Ifenyinwa coming back home, approaching her, and they exchanged pleasantries. She inquired of Anulika, but she lied to her that she has gone to school while the poor orphan was at the farm that early morning working. She was happy her friend's daughter has gone back to school gave her the gifts she brought for her and left. Mama Ifenyinwa became annoyed.

"Why should she bring food items?" She inquired. "Is she trying to show we don't feed well in my house or something else?" She said as she took the gifts and threw them inside the bush.

It was Eke day; Mama Ezekwesiri was coming back from the stream with a bucket on her head. She met Anulika who was supposed to be in school by that time going to the stream to fetch water. Anulika greeted her. She stopped and inquired why she has not gone to school by that time. It amazed her when Anulika told her she stopped school the day she lost her mother. Mama Eze recalled how her aunt told her she was in school. She also inquired to know of her well-being. Anulika did not hide anything from her as she told her everything that happened ever since she started living with them. Mama Eze later promised her that she'll tell her husband's sister at Enugu town to come and take her. She once told her that she needs a young girl. Anulika was happy on hearing this. She heard from people about opportunities in the city. She thanked mama Ezekwesiri for being kind to her and they both went their separate ways.

* * *

A day after, Mama Eze came back to Ikeobi's house, it was in the evening, Mama Ifenyinwa took the goats to the place they usually keep them when she arrived. The goats were bleating continually as it kept dragging mama Ifi but she over powered the stubborn goats. She stood waiting for her to tie the goats and come out. She came out dusting her hands, they exchanged greetings. She went in and brought out a bench, motioned to her to sit down. She tucked her gown and sighed "*Ewo!*" as she squatted to sit down.

"You are welcome," said mama Ifenyinwa.

Mama Eze waited; she cleared her throat and told her why she has come to see her. On hearing this, she became so aghast, but she ran in thought and said within herself.

"If I refuse, they'll say I do not want the daughter of my husband's brother to go to the city. They can even go as far as saying I decided to keep her as a maid," she said. "I know people of Amagwu and how sluggishly they think," she included. With a stellar smile on her face, she asked "When is she coming to pick her?"

"I wanted to get your consent before sending for her," said Mama Ezekwesiri as she smiled. "Maybe in three days' time because she told me that she urgently needs a young girl that will be helping her," Mama Eze added.

"Okay now, I've heard you, I'll inform my husband when he comes back," she said.

Mama Eze thanked her; stood up and went home. It annoyed Mama Ifenyinwa because Anulika has been working like a donkey for them. She thought of who'll replace her if she eventually leaves the house. She only accepted to allow her to go to the city because of what people might say. When her husband came back, she told her everything. Her husband disapproved saying that Anulika will never go to the city. She later gave him reasons to allow her to go.

"I know city women; soon she'll come back because she's just leaving from frying pan to fire," she said.

They both agreed to allow her to go to the city believing she'll eventually come back. Anulika was happy when they told her to start getting ready for her travel to the city. She thought of how she'll work hard and complete her secondary education and get her university dream fulfilled.

* * *

Three days later, Anulika was already in the city. It was in Elizabeth's house, the sister to mama Ezekwesiri's husband. They arrived at her one room apartment in Chime Avenue Enugu. Elizabeth was still a spinster in her late thirties. She's tall and curvy though not too beautiful. When they came in, Elizabeth entered the master's bathroom in the house and had a fresh bath. She later told Anulika to bath before resting. Anulika was surprise about how the city looked. She never believed there would be a place like that. Though she has heard from people the city looked beautiful. She promised herself that she must be assiduous enough to excel. They sat at the dining table at the east side of the room eating their dinner. Her aunt told her she'll take her to the place she's to stay the next morning.

"Oh! Thank you, aunty," said Anulika.

"Welcome my dear," replied Elizabeth.

In the morning, she told Anulika to take her bath. Get her stuffs ready so she'll take her to the place she's to stay. She hurriedly took her bath and dressed. They got to the gate, flagged a taxi down and entered. They got to Madam China's shop sited by the roadside in Ogui Road, they alighted. Madam China is a fat but short woman in her late forties. She had a fair complexion that was aided with bleaching cream. Many secretly referred to her as *Ihu Fanta, Okpa Coke* (Fanta face, coke leg). She has a big restaurant, and this attracted both male and female customers. She also has girls she trade for prostitution. Elizabeth held Anulika why they wanted to cross the busy Ogui Road. Madam China sat on a blue plastic chair with her two legs crossed. Her workers were sweeping and arranging the shop. When she saw her friend Elizabeth, she became happy, Elizabeth got to where she sat, and squatted to embrace her. Madam China's legs were too heavy for her to stand up and welcome her friend. She signaled one of her workers to get seat for her friend. She had not noticed Anulika's presence because she did not know her. They were talked about different things why Anulika stood beside Elizabeth. She inquired about her people in the village.

"They are all fine my dear," said Elizabeth. "*Eem*, I brought the girl as promised," she drew Anulika closer.

"Oh my God!" Madam China shouted, "This is an ideal beauty," she said excitedly.

"You can say that again," said Elizabeth. "I heard that suitors have been coming and going for her hand in marriage."

"You mean that?" she inquired, "She's such a beauty that will make everyone that passes her turn head," she included.

"*Nne* what's your name?" she inquired.

"Anulika Ma," Anulika replied.

She soliloquized on hearing the name and later said, "*Eem*, Lizy," she shortly called. "Don't you think the name sounds Igbotic? She'll even scare customers with the name. In this modern world, you hardly see girls with archaic names," Madam China said.

"I agree with you," replied Elizabeth smiling.

She looked at Anulika and told her she needed a change of name because a damsel like her shouldn't be bearing a local name, she included. Anulika was unhappy for having her name changed to a foreign name she knew nothing about. She has always known that name is ones identity and valued like gold. She had no choice than to accept her name being changed to make it right.

"So what name do you have in mind?" asked Elizabeth.

"Sophia, yes Sophia will suit her beautiful face," Madam China said.

They smiled as she told one of her workers to get something drinkable for Elizabeth. At ten in the morning, they closed the shop and Madam China took Anulika to her house. She took her to stay with her, so she'll help with house chores before going to shop and help prepare her children for school.

Chapter Eleven

Two weeks later, Anulika became more familiar with life in the city. Madam China bought many attracting clothes for her, so she'll attract men to the shop. They believed the more attractive your workers are the more men will troop for them. Anulika never liked those clothes that will leave her half naked because she didn't grow up wearing them. She believed it portrays bad image for one to be wearing such clothes. She refused the clothes and told her aunty that she's okay with the one she has. Madam China understood her and kept those clothes. She thought that with time she'll learn to appreciate the dressing pattern in the city.

* * *

One evening, Anulika was serving the customers when Franklin drove in with his red Camry, parked in front to show-off. He's handsome and good body built a customer every prostitute in China's shop wanted to have. Perhaps, he's cute and rich. When he came to the shop, three of the girls ran to him, sat on the blue chair and leaned his head backward. The girls inquired to know who he would want to take but he ignored them. He was continuously gazing at Anulika who hardly noticed his presence, he then inquired who she was. The girls told him she's a new worker. He then sent one of the girls to call her. The other two girls left saying Frank is not a fish of catch that day. When Anulika got to where he sat, she greeted him with a calm and unhurried voice. Frank told her to get a seat and sit down but she refused. She demanded to know what he wants so she can get that for him. Franklin insisted she sits down so they can have a drink and discussion. Anulika pleaded with him and told him to request for other girls in the shop. Frank's temper was flaring as rage boiled through his body. Anulika was such a beauty every man would want to keep by his side. Frank's interest on her was disingenuous and negative. He only wanted to take advantage of the poor orphan and reminded her they are at service and she must obey him.

"Do you know I'm the most trusted client of your madam?" said Frank as Anulika stood in a very rigid posture.

Anulika told him she can't accept his ugly demands and turned to leave when Frank held her back, raised his hand and gave her a sounding slap that drew every attention. His hand stung from the impact as she clutched her cheek in shock and pain, tears welling in her eyes. His hand turned red. Suddenly, Madam China drove in with her blue 406 and parked. Frank was still standing with a frowned face. Madam China came out of the car, took her handbag and walked to her shop. Frank was visibly mad, she inquired to know why he was so embittered.

"Why don't you ask that stupid girl of yours?" Frank said angrily as he bent to collect his car key on the table in front of him and left.

Madam China tried to stop him, but he didn't listen to her as he opened his car and drove off madly. This angered Madam China because she couldn't afford to lose a devoted customer like Frank.

She quickly called the girls and inquired to know who made him that annoyed. When she found out it was Sophia as they call her, she slapped, pushed and told her she wouldn't want to see her anywhere around her shop and home again. Anulika cried bitterly and pleaded with her that she had no other place to go. China gave deaf ears to what she was saying. She took her phone, tried calling Frank, but he refused to pick up. Anulika decided to live as her madam said but was annoyed how her life turned out to be. She always thought she'll live a simple life in the city without problems, but everything was turning the other way around. She decided to go back to Elizabeth's house and tell her she has lost her job. Elizabeth was angry gave her three hundred Naira to go back to the village.

"Go back to the trash that's where you belong," she said angrily.

Anulika pleaded for Elizabeth to let her stay in her house and look for something she can start doing. She bluntly refused and pushed her out of her house. She was walking hopelessly in the street of Chime Avenue. Darkness was already creeping; her own nightmare has trapped her. She has nowhere to keep her head for the night. Going back to Amagwu never came up in her thoughts. She'd rather wander in the street of Chime Avenue than go back to Ikeobi's house where she's forever in a cage.

It was seven in the evening; she was still walking aimlessly when she met with three girls from Divine Love Secondary School Trans-Ekulu. They were boarding school students living outside the school build-ing. They include Maryann, an S.S.I student, Cynthia was in S.S.2 and Juliet was in S.S.I. They live in one room apartment they rented in Trans Ekulu. They came to Chime Avenue for flirting as they call it. She walked up to them and pleaded to follow them home, told them she has no place to put her head for the night. Her story touched them, and they agreed to take her home. They flagged down a taxi and entered. They've eaten to their satisfaction with the men they met in Chime Avenue. They wouldn't think of eating that night. Anulika was hungry and didn't want to bother them again for food. Juliet opened her cupboard when they got home; brought a pot and two Indomies she gave to her.

"In case you are hungry, take this Indomie and cook."

Anulika thanked her and collected the Indomie. Juliet acted as if she has been in her thought. She won't sleep that night without taking anything. She lit the four-corner stove and cooked it. The girls have gone deeply asleep. She ate the Indomie hungrily and later went to bed.

In the morning, the girls got ready for school, Anulika pleaded to stay with them while she finds something she'll be doing to contribute for feeding and paying the house rent. Their facades were kindness, but their bowels were bad attitude. They were kind but lived a rough life. Schooling wasn't their priority. It was like they were forced to go to school. Birds of a feather that met in school became best of friends. They gave her the key to the cupboard and told her to feel at home. When they came home in the evening, they rambled to do their mathematics homework but could not do it. Anulika later found out what they were finding difficult and resolved the mathematics problem. She opted to help them do the assignment. Struck with amazement if Anulika could possibly be intelligent as she only completed S.S.I and S.S.2 mathematics.

"Here's the assignments, if you do not understand it, try so we can receive partial marks from the teacher," Juliet said.

They dressed and went out as usual leaving her at home. She solved the mathematics assignment for them, and they went their way (it's confusing please check.). When they got to school the following day, their teachers praised them for having performed well on the assignment. Their teachers knew they were not bright students but was aghast on their performance. They were the only students in their various classes to have scored such high marks. When they got home, they demanded to know more about Anulika.

"Girl, what class did you stop?" asked Maryann.

She smiled and replied, "I was about to write my junior certificate examination before I lost my mother since then I stopped," she replied.

"Eya," shouted the girls with expression of pity on their faces.

"But girl, J.S.S 3 and you could tackle S.S.I and S.S.2 problem?" asked Cynthia.

"I envy you dear," said Maryann.

She later told them she wanted to start selling pineapple at the holdup, so she'll raise money to start school again. They all agreed to help her with money she'll use to start the pineapple business and they denoted a thousand naira each.

At six-twenty in the morning the next day, Juliet took her to the market to buy some pineapples to sell. When she came back, she got ready and went to school. She peeled the pineapple and sliced it, arranging it on a tray. She took her bath and went off for her business. Anulika sold well that day, when she came back; it excited her that she made two thousand-five hundred naira that day. The three girls were happy and encouraged her to keep going and that her dreams will come true.

* * *

One week later, Anulika was selling her pineapple as usual by balancing the tray pan on her head with a piece of cloth shaped into a ring. She kept walking from one car to another to sell. She was at the other side of the road when a woman in a Lexus, Dr. Mrs. Ajuluchukwu saw her. She happened to be the principal of Divine Love Secondary School TransEkulu; she was a well-educated woman and had supported girl-child education. She sat in her car as she took a steady gaze at Anulika, held her face forward and wondered why a damsel like her hawked when she was supposed to be in school. She honked her horn and signaled for her to come. She ran to sell her pineapple. When she got to the lady she greeted. She inquired to know how much she's selling the pineapple; she told her she sells it at one fifty naira.

"How many remains?" she inquired.

She counted it and replied, "It's remaining fifteen Ma."

She told her to tie the fifteen pieces. She hurriedly tied and gave her the pineapple fruit collected and counted her money. She gave her three thousand naira instead of seven hundred and fifty naira; she returned the balance to her.

"Ma, you gave me more than my pay," she said as she stretched her hand to give her the money.

"Oh!My dear you can keep the balance," said Dr.Mrs. Ajuluchuk-wu.

She became happy, prayed and danced for every day to turn out the same. She thanked her and turned to leave when Dr. Mrs. Ajuluchuk-wu demanded to know why she was hawking when she should be in school. She told her that her story (is or was?) not a roadside story. It would take time for her to tell her why she isn't in school.

"Maybe we talk about it in my office?" she said.

"In your office?" she asked worriedly.

"Yes in my office," she replied, told her to come in the car while she takes her to her office.

At first, Anulika was afraid and rejected the offer but later accepted and followed her to her office.

When she got to her office, she explained to her how she stopped in J.S.S 3 when she lost her mother.

"Girl like you shouldn't be seen on the street," said her. "I wanted to see your parents, but it turned out it's a different story altogether. You sound so intelligent and I won't allow this potential in you to go down the drain."

It excited Anulika because it was like a dream come true for her.

"You will resume school and by tomorrow you'll sit for an entrance examination. This exam will base on J.S.S. 3 work. If you can pass those examinations, you'll write the forthcoming Junior WAEC examination with them next month in June."

It was like a dream for Anulika; she widely opened her month as tears of joy streamed down her beautiful cheeks. She knelt down, thanked and promised her that she'll never regret helping her. She later told her she'll take her to her house, from that moment; she already was a daughter to her.

She asked if she could go home and tell her friends, but the principal refused and told her she'll do it some other time.

It was one in the afternoon the next day, in Divine Love Secondary School, Trans-Ekulu. Anulika had written the entrance exam and was waiting in the principal office for her result to get to the principal. Soon enough, she knocked at the principal's office door, *kpo; kpo*. It was the teacher in charge of the students writing Junior WAEC. She has come with the script of the entrance exam Anulika took. She came in, greeted the principal and handed over the script to her. The principal gave her a seat and she sat down while she went through the marked script.

"Impressive," shouted the principal. She's such a hidden brilliant student, Mathematics 90%, English 93%, Basic science 97%.

"Ma, she is intelligent, this was one of the best scripts I've marked for twenty-five years since I started teaching," the teacher said.

"I agree, she's the best I've seen with this score in our school's entrance exam. Take her once to the office in charge of school uniform. Let them give her school uniform and then see her to her class. She is to be in J.S.S 3A," the principal said.

"Yes, Ma" replied the teacher."

She took her to the office and got her ready for class.

* * *

Two days later, Anulika with the principal's consent went to see her friends. When they saw her in their school uniform, they were terrified, forgot they were looking for her for the past three days. They inquired to know why she has dressed gorgeously with their school uniform. She told them how she met their principal who helped her start a new life.

"We have not even seen you in school," said Juliet.

"Divine Love Secondary School is big, so you won't know or see every student there each day you come," replied Cynthia.

"Nevertheless, we're happy for you. At least your dream is becoming a reality," said Maryann.

She thanked them for taking her in even when they knew nothing about her. They were happy and they talked at length before Anulika went back to school, so they'll.

* * *

Two months after the Junior WAEC examination, the result came out and Anulika made straight A's. Because of her performance, Divine Love Secondary School became the best school in Enugu that year. On Monday morning when all the students came back to begin the new academic session, the principal welcomed them officially. She brought Anulika before the students and announced to them that their school won the best academic award this year because of her performance. She challenged other students to emulate her and be studious so that Divine Love Secondary School will attract the attention of the government.

"Hard work pays," she told the students as she ended her speech.

* *

Anulika was now in S.S.2 and ready to select subjects for her senior WAEC the next year. She opted for sciences, though was good in both science and Arts. She went for science because of her passion for discovery and innovations. One of her friends Cynthia has written her senior WAEC examination. She didn't make it because she left Divine Love Secondary School to Miracle Center. Students in Divine Love Secondary school are required to have all their papers with A's and B's. She regretted registering with the Miracle Center that year. Juliet and Maryann were then in S.S.3 but planned to leave school once the registration starts. Anulika advised them and they were wise enough to heed to her advice. They wrote the senior secondary school examination in Divine Secondary School and they cleared their papers.

It was time for Anulika to write her Senior Secondary School Examination (SSCE), she became too studious as she started early because she knew the brain needs time to subconsciously digest everything you put in it.

"Many students fail to pass because they rely on last minute cramming. I must avoid such reading habit," she said.

* *

One afternoon, she was in the sitting room watching television. The sitting room is large and rectangular. The focal point is a huge fire place containing a cast iron wood burner and logs. It's attractive and looked modern as the house is only about 8 years old. Pictures on the wall were cool. It has a big plasma TV mounted on the East side of the wall. She sat on the three-seater comfortably, held a small pillow on her lap. Soon, the principal came in and sat on the seat next to the threeseater. She told Anulika to get an orange in the refrigerator for her. She stood up, drooped the pillow she carried went in and brought the orange on a shiny ceramic plate, drew a side stool closer to her and kept the plate on top of it and went back to her sitting position. She took one of the oranges, sliced it and started sipping it. The principle called Anulika by name and inquired to know how well she has been preparing for her senior secondary school certificate examination. She told her that she has been making the best preparation.

"Have you seen this year's JAMB brochure?" asked the principal.

"Yes, Ma," she answered.

"The JAMB registration has started, and I would want you to register as soon as possible. So have you given a thought to the course you want to study and your school of choice?" she inquired.

"Yes, Ma" she replied, "I have been longing to tell you, but you seemed too busy with the WAEC registration that's going on in school," she added.

"Oh my dear! I'm so sorry, each time you want to see me; I want you to come even though I'm preoccupied," she said as she smiled, later asked her the University and course she'll opt in JAMB.

She told her that her first choice University (is or was?) Ebonyi State University, Abakaliki and Applied Biology as her undergraduate major. At first, the principal didn't want her to study in Ebonyi State University neither would she want her to study the undergraduate course she has opted. She told her she would want her to choose University of Ibadan and go for Medicine and surgery since her only daughter is also in her third year there. It will be helpful for her. She will put her through some courses.

"Do you know University of Ibadan stands out? Best sort for all intelligent students. Besides, medicine and surgery suits your personality," she advised.

She told her aunty "Biology is the most mysterious discipline left on the planet. I feel biology will fine tune my research abilities. I have a quest in mind and biology is the perfect fit. Life is still more complicated than anything humans ever built. It's a subject to study and can lead on to various rewarding career paths."

"Interesting!" she shouted, "I've seen that your reason is so strong, and you'll excel if you should take this course up. But I insist you choose University of Nigeria Nsukka because they're good in biology and have good structures. So come to think of it, there are no structures in Ebonyi State University," she said inquisitively.

"Ma, I think I like the school," she replied.

"Don't just choose a school because you like it," she replied. "Go, join the lions and lionesses. What's so special about this your Ebonyi State University? Tell me."

"On careful study of the Ebonyi State University website, I found out that their biology program suits my needs perfectly and active research is in accordance with my interest together with its eminent faculty excellent research facilities, pleasant university ambience and balanced academic program. I feel that EBSU is right place to embark upon my undergraduate study. However, I believe enrollment in EBSU will satiate my thirst for the subject and provide an opportunity to scale the ladder of success. I think it's high time we started looking beyond structures while choosing a University and consider the University that will bring out the best in us," she said smiling.

"Bravo!" the principal exclaimed, "You made the right choice, I'm looking forward to welcoming you as a research professor and I must see to it," she said happily.

"Thank you for believing in me and I promise to make you proud," Anulika said. They continued watching television as they talked.

Chapter Twelve

She sat in her office holding some papers in her hand, held her face forward as she cast a steady gaze at the paper in surprise. Soon enough, the office door open-and-shut; its creaking noise brought a chill to her spine. It sounded like some dying animal, crying out its pain and sorrows with its last breath. She walked to the principal.

"Ma, you sent for me?" said Anulika.

"Oh, sit my dear," the principal replied.

Tensed waiting for her to let the cat out of the bag. The principal looked at her with a smiling face announced to her the WAEC result is out and she made 8A's and a B. Her acceptance letter has come from her school of choice. She handed the papers to her. She could not believe her sight as tears of joy prickled down her cheeks. The principal stood up and walked to where she sat, held her by the shoulder.

"My dear, you've made me and the school proud. I pray for bigger success as you start your undergraduate journey."

Tears were still dropping from her eyes like water. She raised her head and looked at her aunty who bent low as she held her on the shoulder, thanked her for having brought her thus far and promised to make her proud. The principal embraced her, gave her a white handkerchief she held to wipe her tears.

* * *

Two months later, Ebonyi State University invited every admitted student for the 2004 to 2005 academic session for clearance; the students were excited they'll be joining the University soon. First day of the clearance, the admitted students came to clear themselves. The JAMBITES needed to learn how to dress while going into someone's office. Some of them wore slippers. Some wore shorts with a military buzzcut, prickly to the touch. Anulika also came to clear herself. It wasn't easy for the students. They had to go through a long queue to see the faculty officer to clear them. Clearance for science students was in PRESCO Campus where the students came in and out. The newly admitted students were still so naïve because they hardly knew the difference between faculty and department while they were filling their form. Most of them were filling faculty in place of department and department for faculty and vice versa.

The older students were also busy looking for first year students to confuse. It's an unwritten law in the universities for the male chaps. Whenever they have new intake, they quarrel with their so-called campus couple. They believe they're outdated as they parade like a sheep without house looking for the JAMBITES.

It was about ten in the morning on the PRESCO Campus, the campus was busy as students were busy running for lectures, while others just finished from lectures and were going home. Some were at the medical center, a restaurant in PRESCO Campus taking drink and playing games. The photocopiers were running around looking for students who want to make photocopies of handouts, documents or other relevant papers. The newly admitted students were still on their clearance. At the love garden situated in front of the lecture hall called Fans Hall behind CO1 lecture hall for 100 level students, seated four male students. There were nine molded seats and trees at the middle to give it shade. The students sat as they talked. The four students were Samuel who wore polo, a white short and a brown timberland shoe. He's average in height and dark skinned with an afro cut. His nickname is Ozone a 300-level student of Biochemistry. Seated next to him was Ebuka who is of average height and slim, wore blue jeans with several design and flat canvas, known as Buskin, a 200-level student of Applied Biology. Sixtus was short and plump, wore a plain trouser, short sleeve and black shoe. He stood with his bag hung on his back and is a 300-level student of Applied Microbiology. James who sat at the edge of the molded seat is tall and average body built, has a low cut and known as boss. They sat as they talked. They couldn't stop admiring the new entrants. They kept talking about them as Buskin told them he must do everything within his reach to get a chick (as they refer to girls) from the JAMBITES. Ozone inquired to know what he'll use Ifeoma his girlfriend for knowing too well how she loved him.

"Damn the love," replied Buskin, "she's outdated you know," he said as they burst out laughing.

Soon, there came a paragon of beauty whose beauty cannot be interpreted with just a grade 12 English. She was gorgeous and stunning as she walked majestically on her blue trouser and pink shirt, hung her bag on her shoulder. When she walked past the four students, they paused their lips as they strain their necks at her beauty.

"Guy; this baby turns head *o*," said Buskin as he stood up from where he sat.

"*Omo*! The girl too hot," said Ozone.

Buskin could not hold himself, "I must talk to her. *She get am and she be the kind girl wey I want.*' Buskin said in Pidgin English which was their language of fun. A verbal jazz of broken English interspersed with other Nigerian languages and a good dose of gesticulation.

They wished him luck as he walked to meet her. When he got to her, they exchanged pleasantries. He knew too well she's a first-year student devised a means which he would use to get her. He inquired of her department. He was aghast when she told him she was in the department of Applied Biology. With his mouth opened to his jaw, he shouted, "Damn it."

Anulika tried to know why he was so astonished on hearing her department.

"Nne, you're the way too beautiful, but you see that department you just mentioned now, they go drain you," he said.

He was confusing her more with words, she needed people that will get her encouraged but was only seeing those scaring her.

"Sorry, but what do you mean by drain me?" she inquired.

"Applied *gwo-gwo*," he said smiling. "I'm a 200-level student of the department, am sorry to ask, what was your JAMB and POSTUME score?" Buskin asked.

"I made 330 in JAMB and 348 in POSTUME," she replied. "What?" He shouted surprisingly, demanded to know what brought her to Applied Biology Department with such score.

She told him that she loved Biology and would want to venture into a career in biology.

"And you choose Applied biology in EBSU?" inquired Buskin surprisingly.

"Yes of course, is anything the problem?" she said.

"Didn't you see UNN? Didn't you see UNIBEN? Na EBSU you come suffer, "Oh! What make you talk so ill of your department? Tell me, are the lecturers not friendly? Don't they come for lectures?" she asked.

"*Eem*, can you ping me your digit may be when next we see we talk about it."

Anulika who was still new to the system didn't understand what he meant by digit, she asked him what a digit is.

"Oh! I forgot that you're JAMBITE, I mean your phone number."

"For?" she asked

"I want to help you get every material that you'll need in your first year because I've them at home. When I get home and arrange them, I'll ping you."

"Oh! That was thoughtful of you, sorry but I do not need them, see you some other time," she said as she turned and walked away.

Buskin's friends started making a mockery of him because he didn't get the number as he boasted. It annoyed Buskin and he left them but promised t he'd do everything possible to get her.

Anulika finished her clearance within three days got to know two female friends in the course of the clearance. They were Martha and Queendaline. Martha is in the department of Biochemistry while Queendaline is in department of Applied Microbiology.

After the clearance, some newly admitted students started with tutorial classes. Many tutors trooped in and out to teach them and extort money from them. Most of them were selling round off books in different courses. Anulika was not among the students tricked to buy those rounds off texts because each time she saw it, she kept thinking of how one can possibly round off a book of 300 to 500 pages. The lazy students spent much money in buying that round off books because they found it difficult to sit and read other bulky books from school. The tutorial masters created fear into most of the students each time they came, by repeatedly saying that students hardly pass. "Do you see MATH 101 and 102, BIO 101 and 102 and the ICH courses, they are the courses students fail the most. No matter how intelligent you think you are. It's either they give you a D, Pharo let my people go as they call it, or you join the queue of carryovers, especially in BIO and ICH department," one of the tutors said to instigate fear in students.

This worried students the most. Anulika promised to burn her midnight candle as never before because she would break the record. When they finished with tutorial classes that day, Buskin stood at the corridor of the CO1 hall waiting for her to come out. When the students started coming out, his eyes started going far and near in search of her. There were too many students to pinpoint but luckily for Buskin, he saw her as she was coming out with her two friends. He ran and approached them as he continuously shouts.

"Excuse me."

When he got to them, they exchanged pleasantries and he requested to talk to Anulika privately. At first, she bluntly refused but her friends told her to listen to him first and know why he wanted to see her. She agreed and they took about five to six steps backward. Anulika stood with open arms as she stood tall in certitude listening to him. She asked him how he managed to see her when there are too many students coming out of the hall.

"Bae maybe you don't know but your beauty radiate like that of the sun. It's easy for one to get you noticed in the crowd," he said smiling.

She was getting uncomfortable with everything; she demanded he talked so she won't keep her friends waiting. He deepen his hand into the bag he crossed on his shoulder, brought out some lecture materials, and stretched his hand to give it to her. She rejected it and warned him to stay away from her. Buskin pleaded with her to just accept him as a friend but before he could finish talking, she walked away and left with her friends. Standing in the field near CO1 hall were Buskin's three friends as they lay in watch to see how the drama would go again. They kept laughing at their friend why he was unhappy for his unsuccessful mission. He swore never to allow Anulika rest until they become a campus couple.

* *

Four months later, they wrote their first semester exam and went on semester break. Before they went for the break, Queendaline gave Anulika's number to Buskin when he asked for it but told him never to let her friend know she was the one that gave him the number.

* *

Two weeks later, while they were still on break, Anulika was in the sitting room watching television with a pillow on her lap. Her phone was on the side stool, near the two-seater she sat on, soon enough the phone rang, she took the phone, looked at the screen but it was an unknown number. She decided to pick the call. To her surprise it was Buskin who called, she couldn't wait for him to say a word then she hung off. Buskin became infuriated, but he believed in his guts and sworn never to let that beauty pass him by. She kept the phone and continued with the television as thoughts were running through her mind of who gave her phone number to Buskin. No sooner than later, the phone rang again, she ignored the call. It rang the second time; she picked it and shouted, "What do you want?"

"Oh!" said her course representative who was the caller this time, "Anulika, is me your course rep," he said.

"Ah! Course! Course! Course!" she shouted happily.

"Seems you quarreled on the phone? What's the problem?"

"It *Is nothing coursy, na one 200 level student who no won me make I rest*," she said in pidgin English.

The course rep smiled, told her she's just stunning and every guy on campus would want her to be his chick. "*Eem, Anuli, e get wetin I call make I yan for you*," said the course rep in a low and unhurried tune.

"*Wetin be that coursy*? Hope no problem?" she replied.

"*Problem dey o, but no be big problem shaa,*" he said, "Let me quickly go straight to the point," he added. "*Na* school matter, you know how tough our department is? One needs to gather good Cumulative Grade Point Average (CGPA) in year one before we get to year two where we face those strict and wicked lecturers in our department," said the course rep.

Anulika was still waiting for him to tell her why he called as he continued beating about the bush.

"*Eem, everybody for department don pay o, na am I say make I tell you, so you go pay yours before the man go stop collecting,*" the course rep said.

"*Coursy*, I'm not getting you, please can you tell me what the pay is for?" she replied.

The course rep waited and then he continued.

"*E get six courses wey we discover say e dey sort-able. Plenty people don pay. I don do am for them sharp sharp. As it stands now you failed BIO 101, ICH 101, MATH 101 and PHY 101. Dey come carry D give you for PHY 191. If you won upgrade to A, I go still help you. Because say na you, I go collect 5k for each. I go send my account number, so you pay am this week make I settle everything. Everything na 25k*" he said.

"You *don* finish?" Anulika said.

"What kind question be that *na*?" the course rep replied.

She told the course rep she'll never be part of sorting nor will she use her money for that. She later told him to let her grades be the way they were, "Maybe it's an avenue to put more effort," she said.

"*So you mean say you no won do am?*"

"Yes," replied her. "O girl you get mind *o*." "Thanks!" she replied.

The course rep hung the phone annoyed because he could not trick her into paying the money. When he called Queendaline, she was afraid but confused when the course rep told her BIO 101 was among the courses she failed. She doubted BIO department is sort-able. She heard from older students the lecturers are strict. They have many professors that can never engage in such an unlawful act, but she naively paid it, so she'll never fail any course because she was so afraid of carryover.

"Carryover in EBSU? When'll you clear it?" she said to herself.

* * *

After three weeks, they resumed school. Queendaline and Martha went to Bethel hostel to see their friend Anulika. Bethel hostel is close to school. It has 76 rooms. Anulika preferred a hostel that's close to school because she wanted to be attending lectures early. When they came in, Anulika was on top of her bed listening to music with her phone, an ear phone connected to the phone and fixed to her ear. Queendaline and Martha Knocked and became tired of knocking, deciding to open the door and go in. When they went in, they saw while Anulika refused to hear their knock. They sat down as they exchanged greetings.

"*Girl you don fat finish o,*" said Queendaline to Anulika.

They were still talking when Anulika's phone rang, *brr, brr, brr.* She picked the call to know who her caller was. The caller told her that she's Juliet, she never knew anybody that has that name but inquired if they have met. Amazed, it was her friend Juliet from Divine Love Secondary School, TransEkulu. It amazed her and she asked how she managed to get her phone number. Juliet told her she stumbled into her on Facebook though she hardly recognized her, but she followed her intuition and it later turned out to be right.

She inquired of Juliet's where about.

"I'm studying business administration in Delta State University Abraka," said Juliet

"Wow!" shouted Anulika as she jumped out of the bed and walked towards the window.

"Which level you *dey*?" Anulika inquired.

"I'm in my 200 level and preparing for first semester exams," she said as she smiled on the phone.

"Exams?" she asked inquisitively.

"Yes exams, we are fast," she replied

"You guys have not started exams?"

"*Omo*, we are just resuming for the semester," she said.

"Which school be that?" she asked.

"*Na* EBSU *o*," she replied

"*Hum*, EBSU too dull o, they should be fast na," she added.

"*Nne na* how we take see am," said Anulika.

She later inquired about Juliet's well-being. She told her she has been doing well. And thanked her for letting her know that education pays when they were still in secondary school. "I know say na 100 level you *dey baa*?" asked Juliet "Yes dear," Anulika replied.

"Have you seen your first semester results?" asked Juliet

"Result *ke*? I hear say EBSU result *dey* show one week before they start exams," Anulika replied.

"*Hum*! Not good *o*, people wey get carryover go carry bad mind go write exam," Juliet said.

"We pray they reshuffle the academic calendar and meet up with other schools and release school result two or three weeks after exams," Anulika said.

"I trust your guts, I know say your result will cry with A's," Juliet said as she laughed over the phone.

"Nne stop flattering me, EBSU no be *moi moi*," she replied.

Juliet told her lecturer has entered class; she hung the phone and promised to call back after lecture. It excited them speaking after a longtime. Her friends inquired to know who she was. She told them it was one of her old friends back then in secondary school. She brought out some oranges for her friends in a stainless plate. They ate the orange as they talked and laughed.

* * *

Two months after the second semester resumption, their first semester result came out on the notice board. When Anulika checked hers, she cleared her papers with straight A's and a B, her Grade Point Average was the best in the department. Queendaline made 3A's, 3B's, 4C's, and a D, the Pharo let my people go she had was in Mathematics and it was a 3-credit unit course. She was very annoyed and hurriedly went to the course rep to know why she got a D in Mathematics after sorting it. When she got to him, he was in his house drinking a bottle of Gulder. She squeezed her face and was ready to collect her six thousand naira from the course rep. the course rep offered her a seat, but she refused to sit. He inquired to know why Queendaline has come to his house with an unhappy face. She burst out shouting, "I got a D in mathematics after sorting it?" she said angrily.

"Oh! You suppose to come here with some bottles of Gulder to thank me," he said. "The lecturer refused upgrading your score because you failed woeful beyond mark addition, but he managed to give you a D after much pleading and I gave him seven thousand for that particular one. You suppose to balance me one thousand and here you are ranting," the course rep said with a moody face.

Queendaline pleaded for having acted the way she did. The course rep accepted her pleas and promised to make the second semester result look better than the first semester. She thanked him and left happily that she didn't get any carryover.

Chapter Thirteen

Six months later, Anulika is now in her 200 levels. It was the second week of resumption. The students of the Applied Biology Department 200 level sat in the biology laboratory. They were talking with friends that sat close to them waiting to receive their first lecture for the semester. Soon enough, the lecturer came in and the students kept quiet when they saw her. She climbed to the podium for the lecture, greeted the students and they responded. First, she decided to welcome them back to the new semester and applauded them for having made it to 200 levels.

"Applied Biology no be *moi, moi*" said the lecturer. "If you don't take your time, you'll spend number of years here without certificate on which the university will thank you for patronizing them," she said.

The students started murmuring as she said that. She didn't mind their noise, she continued with what she was saying. It annoyed her when the noise echoed more than she can bear.

"You are now claiming to be big boys and girls?" she said as anger crept in her voice. "Mind you, this is year two and not year one where you wrote objective questions and managed to pass. No one ever made A in my course; if you're an average student you cannot pass my course," she said angrily.

The students with fear kept quiet. Anulika was worried when she said that no one has ever gotten an A in her course as she stood up and asked her, "What if the student wrote well? Is there no possibility of making A?" she asked her with expression of worries on her face.

The lecturer explained vividly that no student has written to impress her. She told them she's insatiable when it comes to academics.

"Maybe you need to ask your senior colleagues about the department you are into," she said. "I'm not trying to scare you but you must be very studious so you can leave this school with 2.1 or at least with 2.2," she said. She later introduced her topic and left while the students left still talking on what she said during her introduction.

* * *

Three months later, they were about to start their first semester exams, Anulika was so nervous. She read as never before because she needed to satiate the lecturers test. After writing the first semester exam, most of students were happy saying they passed the lecturers assignment. Some claimed they're more intelligent than others. They showed-off in classes, when the result came out, they became down to earth because the assignment they thought to have given the lecturers bounced back on them because they had many courses they'll be writing as carryovers. Indeed, Anulika's performance that semester was so awesome. The students became envious of her success. She later broke the record of making A in those courses the lecturers seemed strict when marking, her GPA that semester was 4.92.

* * *

Some months later, they resumed for second semester. The three friends sat at the love garden at the back of C01 hall. They were talking; soon, the students sharing fliers interrupted them for the Faculty Association of Science Student election. They came with the fliers and some gifts to buy the students mind voting for their candidate. They told them that Ezaka Ifeanyi is in the department of Applied Biology and from Ezza. They told them to cast their votes for him gave them the flier and sweets. Anulika refused to collect the sweet; quickly Martha grabbed the sweet candy on her refusal. The students left and went to other students. She later inquired why she refused to collect those sweet candies,

"This is what you'll benefit from them. Once they enter the office, they turn to something I do not know," Martha said.

She told them they won't buy her vote with a sweet candy or even the most expensive gift on campus. Queendaline told them his brother is also out for the FASSA President.

"You are from Izzi now Martha?" she said laughing.

"Have you forgotten that I was the one that shared his matchbox for the students day before yesterday?" Martha replied "Oh! My little brain has forgotten," Queendaline said.

They told their friend Anulika to help them get every guy in campus to vote for their brother from Izzi since they are trooping in for her. She told them to keep ethnic sentiment aside and vote for the right person.

"Senti gini?" Queendaline asked, "abeg pack that sentiment of yours one side. If I vote for all these Ezza students what will I gain from them?" she said angrily.

She tried to persuade them to make the right choice before they will embark on a journey they'll regret. They both bluntly refused saying that Izzi nneodo must be the president. This departmental ethnic sentiment had become order of the day in Ebonyi State University. Students are voting simply because they're from the same local government. Maybe they're from the same department. It turned out at the end of it, the president elect, and his inner caucus offers nothing. This is simply because they're not leadership oriented. Anulika tried to advise other students that came to her to vote for the right candidate to do away with political fanatics, but it never turned out well.

* * *

A day later, some final year students were in their class after their first lecture talking. They are in the department of Applied Biology.

"It's unfortunate that half of the students in our level may be coming back for spillover," the course rep said.

"*Coursy*, you're right o and the department is not helping matter," said one of the course mates.

"We're already in final year. It's impossible to correct any mistake we would've made in our first, second and third year respectively," another classmate said.

It's unfortunate the students have enough credit loads they needed to clear. They're fading up already because they knew they'll be coming back for spill over.

The students claim they worked hard but after, their efforts will go down the drain. They've always put blame on their lecturers. One of the intelligent students told them that some of the problems they face might be struggling to study medicine when they're still in Applied Biology. Passion to study Applied Biology is not there. They found out at last they've made much mistakes they wouldn't correct. "I'm not trying to say we don't read. There may be possibilities we have ourselves to blame and there're possibilities we may've the lecturers to blame," she said.

Chioma by name stood up angrily and asked, "What of the lecturers that come to lecture just two weeks before exams? Does it mean they don't know there're students that are not fast enough in reading, they expect one to grab their bulky handouts and get enough information in them."

The course rep later told them they need to sit together and put those challenges to paper and have it submitted to their Head of Department (HOD). So other students won't suffer the same problem. They got up and left angrily.

She dressed gorgeously in a black suit though a trouser, a white shirt that was dazzling. Her heels were not too high, and her long black hair neatly packed hung over her shoulders like a curtain. When she passed, people around her will gradually succumb to the mystic languor exhaled by the perfume she wore. She moved with grace and elegance, so poised and beautifully made. She walked into the lecture hall. Her heels were emitting some sound when she matched on the floor, a sound that attracted the attention of every student in the lecture hall waiting for the lecturer to arrive. They strained their necks starring at the beauty to behold as she walked majestically to take a seat at the third pew by the window side. They had GST class that day, general class for the departments in sciences. The students started wagging their mouth gossiping why she should be dressed for the science class.

"Why doesn't she go to medicine or law if she wanted to show how to dress?" said the students.

She overheard some students near her say the same, but she ignored them. Soon enough, a man who gorgeously dressed came in. The jacket he wore over his broad shoulders had neatly polished buttons and scarf round his neck tied so the ruffles filled the space left open by his coat. When he walked to the podium, the students took a lasting gaze at him murmuring, "It is like today is fashion day? Nobody had cared to tell us so we would also be on our own outfit," they said as they burst out laughing.

The man motioned at them to stop making a noise while he spoke to them. He told them the school sent him to come and select the best dressed, most gorgeous student who'll be going to Abuja to represent the school as Face of Universities. He told them he had been to Campus of Agricultural Science (CAS), Ishieke and Permanent site but the girls dressed odd to school.

"It's your turn PRESCO," he said.

They didn't allow him to finish as all fingers pointed to the gorgeous and stunning damsel that came in embarrassed. The man motioned to her to come up the stage. She walked with her shoulders well relaxed as she cat walked to the stage, made all heads turn. It impressed the man and he gave her few minutes to speak to other students. She smiled with an attracting dimple on her chin.

"Great Nigeria students," she said.

"Great," echoed the students.

"I am Udemba Anulika by name, a 200-level student of Applied Biology. The students interrupted her as they shouted, "Hey! *Gwo! Gwo!*"

She paused her lips and later continued. "When I came in, I became embarrassed by the way my fellow students stared at me. I even heard them making *jest* of me. It didn't move me, Kenji Miyazawa would always say that "we must embrace pain and burn it as fuel for our journey, you're addressed the way you dress, your department should not be an avenue for you to start dressing the way you'll not sell yourself good, thank you."

Her courage bolstered the students which made them gave her a clapping and a standing ovation. She touched the lives of students that do not like their course of study. The man took her to the senate. The senate congratulated him for having done a good job. Anulika became

Face of EBSU and the Face of Nigerian students in tertiary institutions when she got to Abuja.

Chapter Fourteen

Ten years later, Anulika married after her P.HD. A first-class in B.Sc., first-class master's degree and a distinction in P.HD but she could not boast of a white-collar job in Nigeria. With the Myriads of knowledge she has, she went to interviews to both government and private establishments but her academic abilities intimidated the interviewers. They denied her the work simply because they always fear she'll struggle for their office if they employ her. She decided to quit looking for white-collar job. She was married with two children, had a private laboratory which was poorly equipped. Her husband Mr. Okechuku was also a master's degree holder from the University of Nigeria Nsukka graduated with an upper division without work. He managed to be teaching in a private secondary school in Enugu where he receives thirty thousand while his wife Anulika was teaching primary school receiving thirty-five thousand. They were making judicious use of their salary to take care of their two children and solve problems at home. They had a rich neighbor who always scolds his children each time they remind him of obtaining JAMB using Anulika and the husband as an instance of failure after the so-called University degrees. He told them to venture into business where they'll make money than where they'll go and waste money, time and talents.

* * *

For two years, Anulika has been studying a rat in her private laboratory. At times, she dissects and studies the internal structures, at times; it's the external morphology of the rat. The answer why she's analyzing a rat is what she won't tell when asked, though life would've been good for her, if she agreed to venture into modeling when she got a modeling contract in a popular fashion and designing company in Abuja. She rejected the offer because the manager wanted her to use what she had to get what she wanted.

So many girls in her shoes succumb to the manager's request to get famous. Her life was different because she chose to be poor rather than use herself for money.

* * *

One afternoon, when they were on a midterm break, she sat on the verandah of their house. It's a self-contain house with one room and a parlor. It had a large compound, a black gate. She sat reading a newspaper when a continuous knock at the gate disturbed her. Her two children were inside the sitting room with their father watching cartoon network. She stood, walked to the gate. Struck with amazement by the people she saw. It was Juliet, Maryann and Cynthia. They were looking stunning and attractive in their early 30's. They embraced each other while she took them inside. She went in and brought seat for them "How did you girls locate here?" she asked as she bent low to sit down.

"Have you forgotten you gave me the address when we spoke last week on phone?" Juliet asked as she smiled, "So we decided to pay you a surprise visit," she included.

"Oh no! I forgot I should have gotten prepared," she said as she stood up. "Girls, what can I offer you?" she inquired.

"Anything soft will do," said Maryann with expression of excitement on her face.

She went in and brought three bottles of Amstel malt from the refrigerator gave it to them with straw and an opener. She helped them open it and sat down. They started talking as they were sipping the malt. The three ladies were living a flamboyant life and happily married. What they did not understand was why an academic meritorious student like Anulika would graduate without job.

"Not an ordinary graduate o but a P.HD holder," Cynthia said.

They enjoyed themselves that day after many years they path ways without seeing each other. When darkness started creeping, Anulika led them outside. They hopped in their flashy cars and went home. Anulika's friends having flashy cars did not bother her a bit because she believed she'll drive that car one day.

* * *

Five years later, a pandemic disease from rat started spreading amongst countries. According to the *CNN* news, they believed the disease emanated from bush rats in China. The disease spread through China to Japan, to every Western country and to Africa. It killed 50,000 people, yet to announce more. They named the diseases to be Lassa fever because the first person to become infested ate a rat. The disease killed within three days of infestation leaving sores all over the victim's body. It's believed it was airborne disease. It's Urgent to discover medical cure for the disease. The renowned doctors, physicists tried all they could but to no avail. The U.S Government devised a method of "let every hand on the plough." They announced that every scientist in different parts of the world should start seeking for a cure for the Lassa fever that crept the world; life of all species is at risk. They promised to reward awesomely the scientist that finds a cure to the disease; he or she will enter the world record. There will be a day for commemorating the person. Hearing this, Anulika went wild with joy.

"It's an opportunity to prove to the world biologists are in existence. "It's time to use the wealth of knowledge I acquired in Biology from my undergraduate to P.HD level," she said.

* * *

A day later, she told her husband she wants to embark on a journey.

"A journey?" her husband asked surprisingly.

"Yes, a journey," she answered smiling.

"What journey is that honey?" he inquisitively asked.

"THE ROAD TO DISCOVERY," she said as tears well down her beautiful cheeks.

The husband drew closely to her and inquired why she has decided to embark on such a perilous journey.

"It could be a journey of no return," he said. "Please do not go I've known that you have passion, a dream to save the world but consider the people you're about leaving to a journey with no destination or ending."

She looked at her husband as her eyes were clouded with tears.

"I have made up my mind to end this fracas and no one can stop me," she boldly said. "I leave to Ezza village in Ebonyi state in the next three days. I want to get prepared before going,' she said.

"No problem, if you've made up your mind to do so, who am I to stop your quest? Good luck then," said the husband. He embraced her trying to clear the tears on her cheek.

* * *

Three days later, Anulika left to Ezza for her journey of discovery. When she got to Ezza, she made inquiries of big bushes in the village. They took her to the road that led to the bush. They wonder why a paragon of beauty like her would be looking for a bush. As she walked down the unfamiliar bosky road, she kept looking left and right. The wind roared as the leaves on the tall trees were waving east and north. She got to a point she sat down and rested. Having walked for two days in the bush without seeing a rat to use for her experiment, she decided to end the journey since it was leading to nowhere positive. She walked five poles on her way back and recalled what her mother used to tell her when she was still alive, "a bird sitting on a tree is never afraid of the branch breaking, because her trust is not on the branch but on her wings." "Anulika believe in yourself!" she shouted. She quickly turned back and continued with her quest.

Renowned scientists from different part of the world have also gone on their own quest looking for who wears the crown of a renowned scientist, the best scientist ever lived. The disease became widespread. It has gotten to different parts of Nigeria. Every day, the media announces the death of thousands of people.

* * *

Five days later, Anulika got a rat and started experimenting on the rat with the laboratory equipment she took from her laboratory including the ones she bought from the market on the course of her journey. After ten days of experimenting and no positive result was coming. She also ran out of food; thank God the forest has many untapped fruits because the villagers hardly come to the bush because they're afraid that animals will kill them. She used the fruits for food since she still has some water left.

* * *

One month later, she finished with the practical, got the mixture to present and pray it turned out to be the cure. She was weak, her strength has sapped for going hungry many days. She lay down helplessly inside the bush. Two hunters from the Ezza village known for being fearless, and the only hunters to kill a lion, decided to intrude in the forest that day. Suddenly, they saw the woman lying helplessly. They thought of what might have brought a beautiful lady like her to the bush, but answers were not coming. They later decided to save her from dying. Ikoro, one of the hunters carried her while Egbedike carried her property and held his gun including Ikoro's. They took care of her for three days until she regained her strength. She thanked them and was about going when Ikoro's wife screamed heavily inside the hut, the husband ran in to know what brought about the shout-cry of his wife. When he got in, he couldn't believe his sight, his only son Chidi lay down about given his last breath. Ikoro the strong hunter gave out a shrill cry that brought all the neighbors to his house. Anulika ran in quickly to know what has happened.

"It's Lassa fever," said Anulika

"Lassa fever? What is Lassa fever?" Ikoro inquired.

"It's a pandemic disease that had crept into the world; I never knew it's already in Nigeria." She requested Ikoro should get her a cup. Ikoro ran to get the cup while the neighbours stood with their arms crossed as they gaze in surprise. Anulika told them to leave the vicinity immediately before it starts spreading through the air. Ikoro, his wife, including the neighbours on hearing this ran like a cheetah. She wore her hand glove, covered her nose with two nose masks, poured a little of the mixture into the cup and forced the Child's month open to take the mixture. As soon as the child took it, she stood up with her two hands on her head as she paced round praying for the medication to work. Soon enough, the child wake up and started shouting "Mama,

Papa," Surprisingly, she hugged the child and shouted "DISCOV-ERED!"

The child's father, the mother and the neighbours ran to know what happened. Suddenly, they saw the child who was about dying ran to them and embraced them. They thanked her for saving the life of their only child and later requested she stays back so they can reward her for her kindness towards them. "I have to save the world," she said as she took her bag and left.

At her arrival, her husband welcomed her became happy seeing his wife again after a journey of a month and two weeks or thereabout. He prepared a delicious meal for his wife; she showered and ate to her satisfaction, thanked her husband for being too caring and then had a good sleep.

* * *

A day later, she went to Abuja to present her work to the board of scientists. It was barely one week the delegates sent from the United States of America stopped collecting samples from Nigerian scientists because the ones they collected turned out to be poison and killed the patients instantly. They were preparing to go back to the USA the next day when Anulika came with her own presentation.

"No! No! We are no longer collecting samples from Nigeria scientists, you people are horrible," Larry Randy the director of the board of scientists in United States of America said. She pleaded for them to accept her sample and test. They bluntly refused saying they don't want to complicate issues. After hours of negotiation, Randy accepted to have her samples tested. They took the sample to where the Lassa fever patients were; gave one of them few drops of the sample and waited to see the reactions. The butterflies in Anulika's stomach would pollinate field of flowers as she prayed it worked again. Soon, the patient got up hale and hearty. It shocked Randy and the board of scientists. They later gave it to all the patients, and they recovered. They had her U.S papers prepared immediately. She called her husband on phone, told him she's traveling to U.S.A from Abuja. The husband was happy because he knew his wife's hard work is about putting smile on their face.

* * *

Two days after when they got to the United States, the sample was taken to the laboratory and produced in large quantity. Days later, it got to all nook and cranny of the world with

Anulika's name boldly written on the label. What can she asks for again? They got her ready to speak on CNN. She looked gorgeous again; her face was beaming with laughter. She was about talking to the whole world. First, United State Government told every country for power supply that day for everybody to watch the "world renowned scientist speak to them."

She came on camera, breathed a sigh of relief and sat comfortably.

"My name is Ibe Anulika, from Amagwu village, Igbo-etiti, Enugu State, Nigeria. I'm a P.HD holder. First, I chose to study Biology because of my passion for life. People has always thought it's only medical doctors that save life. Once you are not an average student, your parents and people around you'll tell you to go for medicine. I obtained my bachelor's degree with first-class from Ebonyi State University, Abakaliki, Nigeria. My master's degree, first-class from the same university, I later went to University of Nigeria Nsukka for my P.HD where I came out with distinction. I came from a poor family background. I never allowed the influence of my background to choose the future I was going to live. I'm a P.HD holder without a good work to boast of and my husband is also a master's degree holder, no work also. We have been managing life until this day. I only have this to tell youths out there, in every part of the world, "follow your passion, do not let people chose for you." I discovered myself early and knew a career in biology would take me high and here I am today."

Juliet and her friends were in their different homes watching their friend on CNN as she boldly spoke to the world. They took their phones and started calling one another.

"*Omo, Anulika don hammeram o,*" said Maryann to Juliet on the phone.

"*She no be our class again o,*" replied Juliet.

Her husband was happy as he kept tossing restlessly from one seat to another as he was watching his wife talk on *CNN*. "I must thank the people that brought me this far, on "THE ROAD TO DISCOV-ERY," one person that had inspired me was my mother, the late Mrs. Udemba Nwanyimma, whom

I took after her beauty. I'll not fail to recognize late Dr. Mrs. Aju-luchukwu, the formal principal of Divine Love Secondary School, Enugu and my lovely husband Ibe Okechukwu who has been the source of encouragement. I thank all my friends out there," she stood up and left.

She toured round the whole city in USA. They took her to different parts of the world where she spoke to people. They were happy to meet the only female who singly went on a journey to save the world. Later, streets of the world had a billboard with Anulika standing elegantly with the inscription, "THE ROAD TO DISCOVERY." She got a reward from governments. Is it money? Car? House? What can she ask for? There was a huge price for what she had done.

* * *

A week later, she came back to Nigeria. Nigerian president invited her to Abuja. The president filled with joy told her to name her reward and she'll have it. She thanked the president and told him she only ask for one thing. The president demanded to know what she wants.

"I envision a country for both men and women to stand up and say what they think without ostracizing them for having a real opinion."

The president gave a thought to what she said and granted her request without hesitation.

* * *

Two weeks later, she went home with her foreign engineer with a plan of building a good house in her father's compound. When she got to Amagwu village, the villagers gathered at Ejikeme's compound when they heard that she came home. How news fly! People from their neighboring communities started running on their heels to come and see the world changer. They kept echoing,

"She's a world changer! Welcome the one person that changed the whole world through her discovery!"

She promised them that within some months, Amagwu will become a town. Schools will be built and we'll all support girl child education.

The people shouted

"Yes o!"

Later in the evening, her driver took her to her uncle's hut to greet them. When she got there, she saw the two daughters and the two sons in the hut with many female children, no male. On seeing her, the four siblings started crying, they became ashamed of themselves. They knelt down and begged for forgiveness remorsefully. She forgave them and asked them to sit while they discuss like family. They sat down happily, while she inquired of their mother and father.

"The Pandemic disease you discovered the cure killed them," Ifenyinwa said as she sobs.

The story touched her, and she promised to take care of them.

"What of your husband and children?" Akachi inquired.

"They are fine," she answered. "Eem that reminds me, Ifenyinwa and Nnedi, what of your husband?" she inquisitively asked.

"My dear, we couldn't bear them male children and they sent us out. What our parents did to your parents bounced back at us. Our brothers sent their wives out because of the same problem," Ifenyinwa said as she sobs.

Anulika had pity on them and later told them she'll help them start a good life. They became excited and thanked her for everything. She clambered into the car while her driver drove off.

The End

Bia – come

Nwam – my son

Kedu- how are you

Odimma – it is well

Nnam – my father

Nwunyedim – my husband's wife

O gini – what is that

Amosu – witch/wizard

Nwanyi – woman

Aru – abomination

Ehe – exclamation

Ogbono – bush mango

Nnoo – welcome

Taa Kpuchie onu – come on, shut up

Igwe – king

Achi – *Brachystegia eurycoma* (Harms)

Anu nchi – squirrel meat

Nne mama ya – the daughter of her mother

Ukwunnu – a derogatory remarks

Ehem – exclamation

Cha Cha Cha – informal greetings demonstration (by Igbo people)

Iyaaaa – response

Ndibe anyi kwenu – my people I greet

Eeh nna anyi – answer to call (especially a wife to the husband)

Ndewo – thank you

Ezigbo nwanyi – good woman

Dashiki – a loose britly colored shirt (Yoruba language)

Nwanne adi na mba – no brother in foreign land

The Road to Discovery

O ginikwa na ututu a – what is it this morning

Kukuku – sound made to clear the throat

Ofu mgba – one play

Uri – Igbo make up

Uhie – cam wood

Nzu – chalk

Ezinwanne – good sibling

Daalu kwa – well done

Nne idi okay – girl you're beautiful

Umuokorobia Akpuato ha ana ahukwa uzo – is Akpuato men blind

Ezigbo mmadu – good person

Nne wepugodu – my dear remove

Ukwa ruo oge ya – there is time for everything

Maka na oburu m – if it were me

Nne lekene m anya – my dear look at me

Nwanyi na agbadazi agbada – I am not getting any younger

Onye no na ulo a – who's in this house

Nne asi m ka m bia mara ka I mere – I come to check how you're
fairing

Ndi iche ibem obu na obughi eziokwu – my fellow elders is it not true

Eziokwu ka ikwuru – you said the truth

O si girl – did she say girl

Nwata nwanyi – girl child

Mbanu dim oma – no, my dear husband

Patch patch ike mpu – a derogatory remarks

Dogoyaro – Neem

Senti gini – what sentiment

Mbanu dim oma – no my good husband

Obi- compound

Tufiakwa – to curse

Gini nwe mezie – what then happened?

Onye abiala be ya na-awa oji – the owner of the house breaks kolanut

Okwa ahia ano ndi Amagwu – it is four market days in Amagwu

JAMB – Joint Admission and Matriculation Board

EBSU – Ebonyi State University

JAMBITES – admission seekers

Omo the girl to hot (PE) – the girl is very beautiful

She get am and she be the kind girl wey I want (PE) – she is too endowed and she's the type of girl I need

Na EBSU you come suffer (PE) – you come to EBSU to suffer

Can you ping me your digit (PE) – can you give me your number

Bae (PE) – girl friend

Na one 200 level student who no won make I rest (PE) – it's one 200 level student disturbing me

E get wetin I call make I yan you (PE) – I called to tell you something

Wetin be that (PE) – what's that

Problem dey o but no be big problem shaa (PE) – there's problem but it's not too much

Na school matter (PE) – it's school affair

Everybody for department don pay (PE) – everyone in the department has paid

Na am I say make I tell you so you go pay (PE) – that was why I wanted to tell you to pay

E get six courses wey we discover say e dey sort-able (PE) – there's this six courses we discovered it's sort-able

Plenty people don pay (PE) – many people have paid

The Road to Discovery

I don do am for them sharp sharp (PE) – I have done it for them immediately

Dey come carry "D" give you for PHY 191 (PE) – they gave a "D" in PHY 191

If you won upgrade to "A" I go still help you (PE) – if you want to upgrade to "A" I will still help you

Because say na you, I go collect 5k (PE) – because of you, I will collect N5000.00

I go send my account number so you pay am (PE) – I will send my account number for you to pay it

Make I settle everything (PE) – let me settle everything

Everything na 25k (PE) – everything is N25,000.00

You don finish (PE) – are you done

What kind question be that (PE) – what type of question be that

So you mean say you no won do am (PE) – so you mean you won't do it

O girl you get mind o (PE) – Girl, you're stronghearted

Girl you don fat finish o (PE) – girl you're too fat

What level you dey (PE) – what level are you

Which school be that (PE) – which school is that

Na EBSU o (PE) – it is EBSU

Nne na how we take see am (PE) – my dear it is how we see it

I know say na 100 level you dey baa (PE) – I know you're in 100 level right

Result ke (PE) – result for where

I hear say EBSU result dey show one week before exam starts (PE) – I heard EBSU release result a week before exam

People wey get carryover go carry bad mind go write exam (PE) – people that had carryover will enter exam feeling bad

I know say your result will cry with "A's" (PE) – I know your result will be crying with "A's"

EBSU no be moi moi (PE) – EBSU is not easy